SWITCHBACK

Blossom and June are identical twins considering a secret lifeswap. But are they identical enough . . . ?

'I can't believe, Bloss, that Randolph won't know in bed.'

'Fucking, you mean?' Blossom was trying to decide which of June's outfits she should wear on the television this evening. It was the continuation of a group discussion that had been started the previous night. An important event, that had been, marking as it did the very first *professional* reversal of the two girls. Blossom had emerged so far with creditable aplomb.

'Yes, fucking – he'll see the difference.'

'I very much doubt it, kid.' Blossom had turned to smile reassuringly. 'You see, the whole success of our sex-life rests on the illusion that I am many different people. It means that he is living out his fantasies, if you like. So that he wouldn't expect me to be the same from one fuck to the next . . . You'll soon get the hang of it. And if you don't, well Randolph will simply assume that your stupidity is just another pose . . . '

SWITCHBACK

Molly Parkin

A STAR BOOK

published by
the Paperback Division of
W. H. ALLEN & Co. Ltd

A Star Book
Published in 1979
by the Paperback Division of
W. H. Allen & Co. Ltd
A Howard and Wyndham Company
44 Hill Street, London W1X 8LB

First published in Great Britain by
W. H. Allen & Co. Ltd, 1978

Printed in Great Britain by
Hunt Barnard Printing Ltd, Aylesbury, Bucks

ISBN 0 352 30263 1

'Identical twins are, so to speak, the "same individual of whom two copies have been printed".'
Larousse Science of Life.

Joan Rostand and Andrée Tétry

For my sister Sally

CHAPTER ONE

Blossom Tree opened her eyes. It wasn't light yet, but she had been rudely awakened (an apt description, she thought) by her husband's heavy erection twitching between her warm buttocks. Nosing its way in like a determined torpedo.

'Bugger me!' she exclaimed crossly. 'I don't know about that!' And sliding over to face him she took his tool in her hand. The firm touch seemed to satisfy the taut, questing flesh; by the time Blossom had drifted to sleep once again, her handful had subsided to nothing.

Meanwhile, some 290 miles away in London, Blossom's twin, June Day, was awakening too. But in quite different circumstances. The man sleeping beside her was a stranger as far as she could tell. She felt cautiously. Circumcised. Nothing much to write home about, neither dressing to left nor to right, but centrally and in the perpendicular – Christ – suddenly there was *heaps* to write home about! She abruptly ceased her sly reconnaissance, having no wish to disturb her bed companion; not before she had had the chance to get her bearings and at least establish where the hell she was. She wasn't at home, that was for sure. This wasn't her bedroom, nor was it one that she had been in before. Yet there were certain similarities to others that she had known, belonging to those of her married lovers.

This man beside her was married. She could tell in the thin light leaking through the thick curtains that this was a family man. The evidence was there; in the nightgown and négligé strewn over the chair and his pyjamas nearby on the carpet; in the extended width of the fitted wardrobes, one openly displaying a costly row of fur coats beyond a plethora of pearled and sequined party wear. This wife was obviously one who enjoyed getting out on the town. Was that where she was now, still whooping it up, but about to arrive back unexpectedly?

June shut her eyes tightly and tugged at her thick fringe. Hell! Hadn't she meant to give this sort of thing up! But last night at Television Tower, events had run away with themselves, ending in a wonderfully boozy blur. Hospitality had been unduly generous with the spirits. She was more used to the frugality of the BBC. Her head ached, but only slightly, not half as much as she deserved. But she was suffering from a terrible thirst and a vague, though not yet troublesome, urge to empty her bladder.

She blinked several times at the bedside table. Someone thoughtful, herself(?), had put down a tall glass of water. She seized it gratefully and drained the whole lot in one gulp, realising too late that it was her vodka and tonic from last night. Instantly drunk, she fell back on her pillow into a state of appalled semi-consciousness. Then mercifully sank into a deep sleep.

When she awoke again it was with a feeling of abandoned gaiety. Rather naughty, yet thrilling recollections of the night before had infiltrated her fleeting dreams. Smudged images surfaced of herself in the centre of an admiring circle of men (consisting in the main of her television colleagues) gradually thinning out to make way for their superiors. Of course, the king-pin would be the programme producer. It was the producer whom June had finally nailed last night, deliberately enchanting him with a stream of light anecdotes, accompanied by occasional smouldering looks geared to lead his thoughts along the same lewd path as her own. She had been fancying this one for months. And then she'd blown it . . . She stretched in the bed, luxuriating in the comfort of the quality linen sheets and the firm base to the hard sprung mattress. Sleeping around and around as she did (as she often delighted in telling people whom she had only just met) made one as much a connoisseur of cribs and couches, as of cocks. She would go on to confide that her favourite was her married sister's four-poster, which was covered in black fur and had sheets of slippery black satin. But this was simply an arbitrary piece of additional information imparted solely so that she would then be asked, as she unfailingly was: 'So you have a married sister – is she anything like you?' Then she would be able to say that she was one of twins. She never felt right until people knew.

Experience told her that this particular mattress belonged to somebody who had a bad back. She had awakened on quite a few of these orthopaedic mattresses of late and could vouch that they gave a damn sight better night's sleep. Not that she was a sufferer, her spine had so far never played her up — touch wood.

Her fingers contacted the smooth veneered surface of the carved bedside table, brushing the empty glass against what she now saw to be a framed photograph of a family. She stared at its focal point, at the pater familias, posing so proudly surrounded by his children. All of them young adults, one even holding a small baby, presumably a grandchild. Yes, that's who she had fucked! The father of them all. This face that as recently as six months ago had been plastered all over the press. The Director General of Universal Television, newly appointed – this very family snap was the one they had run in the *Guardian*. June permitted herself a small self-congratulatory smirk. It wasn't every day a girl landed as big a fish as this, though it was a shame to have had to forego the sexy producer.

A slight stirring behind reminded her that all was not yet over. The Director General appeared in favour of making his presence felt. He was speaking. He was murmuring, murmuring one word softly: 'Cynthia.' June bristled, but not for long, her good humour was such that she was able to forgive the inaccuracy. The poor man was muddling her up with his missus. Next to the family snap stood another photograph, a heavily retouched studio shot of an anaemic blonde whose particular brand of bloodlessness suggested aristocratic forebears. 'Darling – Cynthia', was scrawled across the spray of orchids. Cynthia was without doubt the absent wife.

She turned around carefully; it wouldn't do to move too fast. The Director General was a person of a certain age – not ancient exactly, yet in those hazardous years the heart could, as like as not, do very funny things. The sudden shock of discovering that he was not in bed with his wife might well trigger off an alarming and highly embarrassing set of circumstances. It had happened to June once before. She had found it very frightening, although secretly admitted to a gruesome fascination – she had never heard the death-rattle before. And it was many, many months before she felt sufficiently detached to be able to relate the experience with her customary wit. Of course

3

by the time she had 'perfected' it with several titillating embellishments, the tale did become one of her more hilarious. And she enjoyed the piquancy of dining out on a corpse.

Shit! Now he had seen her – now he'd seen who she wasn't!

Mere inches away from her nose, June was being regarded by a pair of moist, bloodshot brown eyes. The expression was one of puzzled suspicion. She felt as if she'd seduced a St Bernard.

'Good morning,' she said brightly.

The gentle beast blinked, then uttered a low groan sounding more like a bronchial bark; this led to a heaving convulsion of coughing. The bed shook. The brown eyes spun in pivoted frenzy midst an alarming complexion of stretched pores and strained veins. The ham-fists which had lain lightly clasped about her body were now clenched, making mince-meat of her breasts.

'Ah-ha, here we go!' June spoke out loud, voicing her instant and spiralling concern. 'Come on, old boy – enough of all that –' She gripped his hands hard over her swiftly shredding mammaries; and in an ill-conceived attempt to distract him from his bodily paroxysm, she went childishly boss-eyed and stuck her tongue out in his face. It didn't work. Worse, the fierce complexion deepened to a bluish puce. Quite obviously, lack of respect was not much appreciated. Added to which, there now appeared to be a hectic activity down below; the substantial limbs of the Director General were threshing beneath the quilt like a hefty combine-harvester. In two ticks and a tear they'd be buried in feathers, June thought wildly. Babes-in-the-bed, but with a gaping disparity in age. She felt herself to be too young to relish a downy grave. Clearly, direct action was needed to relieve this poor bugger's agitation.

At a certain personal risk to her lush, lissom flesh she lowered herself in the bed and with her capable lips applied the principle of the leech to his parts.

Blossom prepared breakfast, it didn't take long. Her children, Pip and Willow, were away with friends for half-term. She thought about them briefly. 'Little sods,' she said, and grinned. Then she went to the bottom of the stairs and plucked an offensively unmelodious chord on the strings of a free-standing gold harp, before returning to dish up the kippers.

4

The harp was typical of Blossom's rather theatrical style in decor. Though neither she nor her husband, Randolph, were at all musically inclined they possessed, apart from the harp which nobody could play, various decorative instruments including a most striking grand piano which was lacquered a scarlet vibrant enough to dominate any normal domestic interior – but not Blossom's of course. Here it simply merged in the exultant riot of colours; in the vivid pink and crimson of the Mexican rugs on the painted tangerine floor; the brilliant sunshine yellow of the vast dining table – one of Blossom's favourite possessions, the *plastic* table. Purchased in Paris and shipped over to Puddlemouth with immense difficulty and expense, she had claimed it as her tenth wedding anniversary present. The morning it arrived she had let Randolph fuck her on it – free. It was the first time for three years that she hadn't charged.

Upstairs in the spartan austerity of his study Randolph Tree sat reading the *Times Literary Supplement*. He was pondering on an aphorism of Karl Kraus, selected by a Professor Zohn in his recently published *Half-Truths & One-And-A-Half Truths*: 'Life is an effort that deserves a better cause.' Randolph Tree was rather irritated; he wished he'd written it. Added to which he felt unusually hungry. He was used to getting up at six and not breakfasting until Blossom arose, but today found him with a keen edge to his appetite. Pehaps the pervasive smell of kippers had something to do with it. In any event, on hearing his wife's hideous twanging he rose with alacrity. The harp always made him smile; it so exemplified Blossom's beguiling absurdity. Like herself it was an example of impressive grace and beauty, at the same time capable of a discordant note. It was the contrast which led to excitement.

Randolph paused to consider this whilst collecting his reading matter, every single daily newspaper, the *TLS* and the *New Statesman*. And, because she had so pleasured him last night, he had treated Blossom to the new *Vogue*. *Harper's*, *Cosmopolitan*, and *Men Only*. He bet himself that she would choose to look through the *Men Only* first. He heard her shouting to him now.

'Randy – Randy! Come on, you bugger, your kippers are getting cold!' And for good measure she ran what sounded like a fish-slice across the entire surface of the harp-strings. Randolph Tree ran down the stairs, whistling to the diminishing reverberations.

June was late for work, which meant no breakfast again – a fact which didn't worry her unduly. Last night (not to mention her bed-time vodka this morning,) she'd drunk enough calories to last for a fortnight. It wouldn't harm her to cut out food for a bit; the television camera mercilessly magnified every ounce. She was naturally greedy, like Blossom – that was the trouble. They were both forced to discipline themselves, Blossom just as much as June, in order to keep old Randy happy – which was bloody well worth doing, any girl would have agreed on that! June considered her brother-in-law to be one of the most edible men she had ever had; if Blossom hadn't married him she would have done so herself. They had decided that at the time, she and Blossom. It was simply that Blossom had got pregnant first. There had never ever been any hard feelings.

June considered the day ahead. As far as she could tell there was no knowing when she might expect to be sitting down to the approximation of a square meal – sometime after midnight if she managed to get back from Dublin in time. In between now and then, it would be a series of snatched beers and unappetising sandwiches with the sound and camera crew. Not scotch eggs, they always made her fart – a fact which generally embarrassed the interviewee more than herself. Though not necessarily this one. Today's subject was the Irish poet, Connor McConnors who, despite having one foot in the grave, managed to maintain the rumbustious image that had taken a lifetime to cultivate. June couldn't imagine that he'd be thrown off his eloquent balance by the olfactory and audible effects of inner wind.

But before all that started, before she was even due for the final run-through with the director, she had to attend the Female Conference at Media House. At least two extended series on the role of women in society were in the pipeline and the choice of a presenter had yet to be decided. June knew through her agent that she was in the running.

Life was hectic these days, there was no doubt about that. But there was no one to blame; no one and nothing, except her own driving ambition and an inexhaustible appetite for work that made it impossible to say 'no' to new projects. And since she had turned free-lance and left BBC2, where she had irregularly presented the late-night Arts Spot ('irregularly' resulting from the up-and-down nature of her affair with the director), the work had come flooding in. She had appointed an agent, her first surprisingly. Until then it genuinely had not occurred to her that her work, that television, might take over her life. She had supposed that like Blossom she would get married and have children. Viewing it now, in hindsight, that was how she imagined that she and Tiny (the director) would end up – married. Well, married, but both having what they could on the side – the whole set-up a constant and bitter battle to preserve their separate and positive identities, just as they'd been for seven years.

'Bastard!' June swore at the smudged mascara beneath her eye. The desk downstairs had chosen to ring at the least propitious moment. The taxi firm couldn't get a cab to her in under twenty minutes, which would put her bang in the middle of the rush-hour.

'Bastard!' She swore again. It was going to be one of those days. The start of it for Christ's sake was enough of a clue that the gods were seeing fit to exercise their sense of humour at her expense. She had suffered a head-on collision with Cynthia, the blanched wife of the Director General. Whilst June was scurrying away down the stairs from his plush apartment, Cynthia had been furtively sidling up. Both parties, their respective evening attire wildly unsuitable to the hour, had had their eyes firmly fixed on their feet in case of awkward and embarrassing confrontation.

The glitter of Cynthia's sequined dress had stamped itself on June's dazzled retina before she'd had the chance to fully register the woman within. Head bent, elbows flying in the attitude of attack, June had swerved around the curve of the carpeted · staircase at the speed of a soccer international, with no possibility whatsoever of last-minute withdrawal.

Collision was unavoidable; skull cracked against skull.

'Fucking hell!' The strangled expletive from the flailing sequined shape, now slithering swiftly back to base on ground floor, surprised June into a fleeting understanding of what had taken place. The voice so exactly fitted the face in the photograph – high and horsey but with the gritty huskiness of too much gin and cigarettes. The fine wife of the Director General had also been out on the toot!

June had cautiously proceeded in the wake of the poor woman to find her in a state of distressed disarray at the bottom of the stairs, displaying a great area of gusset. June left her whimpering on all fours, autocratically refusing further offers of help.

The memory of the grotesque sight made June wince as she ruefully explored the tender lump above her forehead. 'That's how you'll end up one day, the way you're going on my girl,' she addressed herself in the mirror. 'Arse-holed before eight on all fours in some foyer, but without even a husband awaiting you upstairs.'

The telephone rang again. This time she welcomed the shrill intrusion. The image of her future had fleetingly depressed her. For a bleak second she had felt as lost as she had done in those disorientated months after she had finally split up with Tiny. But it surprised more than disturbed her. It proved that her single state harboured a vulnerability that fought shy of facing the future. This she chose to reject, if not violently then with conviction. In the short time that she had been living alone the most important principle she had learned was that it was not only easier but wiser to live in the present. She optimistically approached each separate day with that in mind. It wasn't that she had any feelings of dread for unforeseeable events – indeed her nature was not inclined toward pessimism – it was more that with Tiny she seemed to have spent so much more time *planning*. Always '*when* we go to such-and-such', or 'we *will* try and do that one day'. Never anything *now*, no immediacy. But that was Tiny's trouble. Now that she was on her own she wasted no precious time on these prevarications. She neither lived in the past or the future, the present offered enough excitement.

She rose to her feet and swung around to answer the telephone, catching sight of herself in the long mirror. It was a fetching reflection, but she viewed herself with the lack of vanity usual to any professional whose appearance is part and parcel of their work. She leaned forward, frowning slightly. To the untutored eye all would have seemed above criticism. The flaming red hair (the previous spring a caramel brown) swung smoothly to her shoulders in a straight, silky cut; the long fringe skimming the darkened thickness of eyelashes. One glowing hair had become trapped between two intertwined lashes and was now actually resting on the sensitive rim of the upper lid and in danger of grazing along the white of the eye. Skilfully, June removed it just in time, narrowing her startlingly green eyes in order to do so. They slanted from her reflection in the mirror. She looked assured and efficient, intelligent and alert. She gave the appearance of being capable and in control, the sort of person able to restore calm to chaos. It was this quality on which her growing reputation was based – an air of relaxed, yet informed tranquillity was rare enough, but in the frenetic world of television it was exceptional. June was, it was generally agreed by those in the know, a girl with a most promising future. (Even at this very moment the Director General was wracking his brains to remember her surname. Before the morning was out he would have put his secretary on the job and made a note in his diary for a luncheon date.) And yet there was something extra, wild and wilful sensuality that lurked behind the shining grape-green of the eyes. On meeting her, strangers had admitted to finding her blazing gaze somewhat disturbing, not knowing that it was many years ago that both Blossom and June had learnt to make use of their remarkable cats' eyes. Hadn't they practised in secret on each other? Not that June ever used her eyes in that special way when she was actually on the television screen. She didn't want to alienate any part of the viewing public, and those sort of looks were specifically meant for men she wished to seduce. It aroused a positive dislike towards her from women. Her sexuality was, from a professional standpoint, something best kept in check. She enjoyed the private reputation of being a much sought after girl, given to distributing her favours where and when her desires dictated. Or, as in the case of last night, when the drink decided – she would not have, if sober, behaved in such an abandoned fashion. After all the Director General was a force unto himself, pursuing a markedly brutal and unpopular policy of hiring and firing in his latest administration. Added to which he was not noted in any way as being a ladies' man. It was the drink, and the snide challenge of the sexy producer that she 'wouldn't stand a chance there', that had made her behave so recklessly. But on the small screens of the nation June showed not a sign of any of these goings-on.

As far as Mr and Mrs Average Viewer went she was suitable to be welcomed into the family home. Just sexy enough for the husbands to think privately that they wouldn't· mind slipping her a length; just friendly enough for the wives to think how nice she would be to have as a pal. And just attractive and fashionable enough for teenage daughters to write in and ask where she had her hair done, and what colour eye-shadow she used. Her public image bore little relation to her private self.

Blossom on the other hand, since she had no public image, suffered very little from this need for camouflage. Her natural flamboyance was reflected in everything around her, not only her furniture and fittings, but even the spot in which she had decided that they should live. Slap-bang in the middle of Puddlemouth's most spectacular surfing beach, theirs being one of the few remaining fishermen's residences midst a complex of crumbling lofts rented out as artists' studios. There was a small inadequate beach café, two monstrously ugly blocks of recently built balconied flats, and a scattering of tiny over-priced, bed-and-breakfast hotels which were only open in the season.

But upon that short, secluded beach stormed the Atlantic Ocean, hurtling its waves against the suppliant sands in a furious effort, so it always thrillingly seemed to Blossom, to reach and demolish the entire line of habitations. As if the mere presence of these frail man-made buildings was an affront to the strength and elemental force of the sea. The noise of the breakers was overwhelming. Indeed when Blossom opened the sliding glass doors onto the verandah the sound made normal conversation impossible. Only at low tide did the threat of the waves recede to a safe though mutinous distance, like a dangerous animal kept barely at bay. Blossom thrived on the continual excitement of the sea. It, more than anything, had been her reason for coming to live in Cornwall. And it happily coincided with Randolph's need for isolation, his wish to be right away from the seduction of the city. But he would have been able to find mental peace as easily in the green depths of the countryside. Blossom felt she might honestly die if she were to be deprived of the daily drama of the sea.

She stood now at the sliding door staring down a   ch

below. This communal floor was the first floor of the house; this was where the open-plan kitchen led onto the dining area, which in turn spread through to the family sitting-room. The sea-facing wall of each floor had been ripped out and replaced with sliding glass doors, all except Randolph's floor at the top of the house which had been converted into his study. He had deliberately obliterated his view, had instructed the architect who had undertaken the conversion to build a false wall over the existing windows, and remove a major part of the roof instead. This then had become his daytime light source. But more than that, it had become his only view. A view of the sky, as variable in its way as Blossom's beloved view of the sea. A blank canvas of clouds suspended over his head, sometimes static and solid, sometimes foaming and free, but forever on the move. Never one day the same. And at night a total change, as if somebody had substituted a completely different painting, transformed by the light of the moon and the stars. Visiting academics who voyaged this far to converse with Randolph Tree seemed always surprised at the sight of the sky-view, immediately jumping to the mistaken conclusion that it betrayed a deep interest in astrology.

Descending the stairs, whistling, Randolph Tree passed the marital bedroom. The door was open. Before closing it he popped his head around, looked quickly into the room and smiled. He was still smiling when he reached Blossom one floor down. But when he saw exactly what she had chosen to wear whilst serving his breakfast he broke into satisfied laughter.

Blossom's love of dressing up was a source of pleasure to them both. Whilst June by the nature of her work was forced to practise restraint over her appearance, Blossom was encouraged by her husband to do the opposite. He thought of June now as he approached the delectable curve of his wife's bare, sunburnt thigh, gleaming against the frilled edge of the tiny white apron. It struck him as odd (whilst relishing the shape of Blossom's rich pubic mound, discernible beneath the fine organza) that for the past few mornings running he had not overheard the twins having one of their animated and seemingly interminable phone conversations. This *was* unusual. Some days they contrived to talk not just in the morning, but in the evening too; he tried hard to resist the crass urge to tot up just how much this recent lack of communication was saving him on the telephone bill.

He had learned a long time ago to accept this unparalleled affinity between the two girls. They were, after all, not just twins but *identical* twins. Monozygotic (identical), rather than merely dizygotic (fraternal). Monozygotic being identical and developed from a *single* egg, as opposed to dizygotic being fraternal, developed from *two* eggs and held to be as separate in their origin as normal brothers and sisters. Randolph had read all the relevant research material within days of meeting Blossom, but he was still unprepared for the uncanny shock of coming face to face with her double.

Both were left-handed. Their hair whorls were identical, each swirling clockwise at the crown of their heads, instead of anti-clockwise. Their palm patterns and fingerprints, their dental irregularities, their complexions, their eye colour – even to the pigment pattern of the iris – all these were exactly the same.

It was unnerving, that couldn't be denied.

But Blossom had warned him that it would be, she had completely understood his child-like consternation. She had smiled, and had humoured him from his sudden feeling of chilling uncertainty. He didn't like the idea of there being two of her, he wanted there to be one. And he wanted all of that one to be all for himself. But it was impossible. Now, even now, almost twelve years later he still found it difficult to come to terms with, just the simple fact that for as long as they all continued to live the girls would continue to be closer to each other than he could ever hope to be with Blossom. She was his wife and more precious to him, almost, than his work. And yet their rich and harmonious intimacy would never transcend the intense bonds which existed between the twins.

Even the fact of Blossom's pregnancy, the pregnancy that had led directly to their marriage, had first been divulged to June. At the time he had resented that bitterly, choosing to see it as a betrayal. But over the years he had learned perforce to forgive and understand. As Blossom had tried to explain whenever he had expressed pain at being second friend and confidante instead of first, it just wasn't like that. He was getting it all wrong. When she shared secrets with June it wasn't like sharing, not like it was with him. When she talked to June it was like talking to herself. A form of 'self-reference' was how she put

12

it. And then she'd comfort him, hold him close to her, enveloping them both with her womanly warmth.

'We were made for each other, you and I.' That's what she'd say. 'This marriage will go on forever.'

And yet, until he had met Blossom, Randolph Tree had honestly never contemplated marriage. Marriage had not seemed to fit in with his plans for the future. He had had many affairs and in almost every case the girls had fallen desperately in love with him and in several cases had even been driven to propose marriage. But Randolph had always fought shy of the notion. Sex was no problem, he was a very attractive man and had always adored women. But his work, his writing, was the most important thing in his life.

He was twenty-eight when he met Blossom, and was about to publish his first book, *The Other Meaning*, a philosophical treatise. His publishers were confident that *The Other Meaning* would capture a world-wide cult readership, at the same time exciting sufficient critical acclaim to assure its commercial success. But no one was more surprised than Randolph Tree when that was what did happen. His economic situation altered, so it seemed, almost overnight. He was free from financial pressure to pursue that which was closest to his heart (apart from darling Blossom). He could give up teaching and spend the rest of his life in study. The study of original thought. And, unless he wished to do so, he need never write another word again.

At the time of his first meeting with his youthful future wife however, his reputation was still unfounded. The occasion was part of the inaugural festivities of the South West Summer Adult Education Symposium. An informal dance was being held, with an extended bar-licence. Randoph Tree was already pleasantly tight. He was a tutor at the Symposium, Blossom was a student from the local Training College. It had been her mesmerising eyes that he had noticed first of all. That and the inviting challenge of her impudent cleavage.

He had said so, in that order. 'You have very seductive eyes and superb bloody breasts – I compliment you on both!' They had stared at each other without speaking.

Then he'd lost her. She had been claimed by a steady stream of men demanding to dance, and he had been left behind in the slip-stream of her lustful admirers. 'Well, that's that,' he had sworn silently to himself. 'You should have known better than to have gone for the belle of the bloody ball.' And he was shocked by the sharp sense of loss.

But she had returned to him.

She returned at the moment that he was taking to the floor for the third time running with a thin and handsome, though slightly haggard, brunette. She reminded him in certain lights of Audrey Hepburn, a film star he had always desired. And indeed he was discovering under fairly discreet and localised pressure that this girl's hard, wiry body was not half bad. Though he had not thought of a way to reveal that the series of lectures on Creative Writing, that she was so looking forward to, concluded with his own withering attack on such writing. He had thought to call critical attention to its gross irrelevance and self-indulgence, pinning the whole thing on Samuel Beckett, but with a massive swipe on the way to James Joyce.

'Of course Joyce is the boy . . .' The brunette was saying. Randoph ran his hand casually between her sharp shoulder blades to check whether or not she was wearing a brassiere. He nodded, she was. 'Ah, Joyce! He is the one all right . . .'

Blossom was standing before him, behind the brunette. 'This is a Ladies' Excuse Me, so excuse me,' she said, tapping sharply on the shoulder of the other girl.

'It most certainly is no such thing!' the brunette began indignantly. 'I definitely heard no such announcement . . .'

'You've heard it now.' Blossom interrupted smiling and kicked savagely at the other's shin. Randolph's fleeting and final impression of his former dancing partner was one of snarling feminine defeat softened only by a wan expression of wincing pain. Blossom was a girl who snatched what she wanted.

Taking her in his arms that first time in the Summer School dance, nine Newcastle Brown Ales pressing on his bladder and conscious of a host of hot jealous eyes upon them, Randolph Tree nevertheless sustained an instant erection. Blossom remarked upon it immediately, but he was to learn pretty soon that this was her way.

'You've got a cock-rise! Oh, goody!' Her candour took him by surprise. 'What's your name?' She spoke with a lilting rush of words.

'It's Randolph Tree,' he answered somewhat stiffly, finding

14

it difficult to concentrate on speech.

'Randy — that's ripe —' She laughed out loud, her head thrown back. He could see extra depths in her cleavage, and to his annoyance was aware that most of the other males around them were straining for a similar view.

They had barely been dancing a few minutes, but he badly needed, for all sorts of reasons, to get outside as soon as possible. He deftly steered Blossom between the leering faces towards the nearest exit. The one he was aiming for he had checked earlier with the brunette in mind. It led directly to the lawned grounds of the establishment, and thence to the leafy perimeter. Though all *he* had honestly intended for that evening, after a pee, was to fondle and kiss. But they had both been carried away by the raw and combustible nature of her passion. It was no surprise when she missed her first period.

'You were trying to bugger me last night.' Blossom undulated towards the breakfast table, her naked breasts breaking free from the restricting bib of the flimsy pinafore. She was wearing perilously high heels which forced her to walk with her shoulders thrown back and her torso arched in an extremely tantalising pose. Randolph could feel the back of his throat tighten up and a distant ache descend to his balls.

'This isn't fair,' he protested.

Blossom stopped moving immediately and looked disappointed. 'Bloody hell, I thought you'd like it — the children aren't here. I was going to make a day of it. We could even go for the record if you're up to it.'

Randolph collapsed into a chair and held his hands over his ears, giving a short, strangled groan. 'Don't say these things, you get me over-excited, then your kippers will give me hiccups. Why not hold on till I've eaten — I mean, keep on walking, I like all that. But keep your mouth shut. Just parade. Don't mention buggery.'

Blossom dimpled, then twirled around slowly. She was not eating breakfast today, she'd decided to cut it out for a whole month (she must remember to tell June that when she spoke to her later, though these days it was getting harder and harder to find her in). 'Your kippers are in the oven.' She presented herself to him in profile, provocatively, with one hand on the curve of her hip. 'I take it I'm allowed to talk if it's about your breakfast?' She approached his chair without waiting for a reply. If

15

he raised his head a little higher he would be able to take a sly bite from the nearside of her luscious breast. Straining further he would be in the delightful position of demolishing the nipple itself . . .

He ground his front teeth together in pleasurable anticipation. 'Get a move on, woman,' he growled. 'I'm bloody starving.'

Blossom flounced past, breasts bouncing, tossing her shoulder-length bob. This summer she and June were wearing their hair in exactly the same shade and style, though they had chosen to do so quite independently, just as before that they had both decided to go caramel brown. Only the colour of her pubic hair, a dark, bosky brown, betrayed the truth; that she wasn't a natural redhead.

Randolph studied her openly whilst sipping his orange juice. 'You're not wearing any knickers,' he observed.

'Do you object?' she said coyly. She had now reached the Aga oven and had to be careful of her state of near nudity against its hot surface. Last time she'd served his breakfast in similarly scant clothing she'd splashed her stomach with scalding Scott's Porage Oats. There was still a nasty little scar in her navel.

'Yes, I think I do, to tell you the truth.' Randolph poured his black coffee calmly, fully aware that his mild criticism would not go down well.

He was correct. She straightened up, the orange oven-mittens on her hands ready to remove his cooked kippers. But he enjoyed the straightening-up process very much indeed, this way he would be getting it twice over. It afforded him a fine view of taut and stretched buttocks; at one moment arched in a high haunch, and the next relaxed and plumped into a pair of firmly filled pillows. In his opinion the gluteus maximus was the most spellbinding muscle in the whole of the human body. He was fortunate that Blossom was possessed of a particularly splendid illustration of this. Her scrumptious bum was a never-ending pleasure to him. He couldn't imagine now what it must be like to make love to an empty-arsed woman, to a girl whose posterior resembled an unfilled paper bag. Though, of course, in the past he had slept with all sorts, those included and they had never disappointed him then – as far as he could remember. Randolph's view of the female reflected his humanitarian principles – so he liked to think. He strongly deplored men who

16

categorised women in terms of their desirability; distinguishing in a disparaging way between the young and the old, or those less blessed with good looks than others. His own tastes were Catholic. All women were a delight to him, a constant mystery and a continuing excitement. It was just that for him Blossom embodied them all — he worshipped at the shrine of her femininity.

'You mean you would rather have knickers *as well* as the suspenders and stockings?' Blossom's glacial green eyes registered her displeasure. She was still standing with her back to him, speaking over her shoulder. Her legs were set wide apart, one supporting her weight, the other, angled away, was bent at the knee for the best balance. The slender shape of each limb was further emphasised by the heavy seam which climbed like a strong pencil-line up the length of her stockings — her tart's stockings, sheer and silky, and sinfully black. With one long sluttish ladder on the inside of the left leg. Randoph could just see its twisted top stretching over her tanned thigh. A sly sensation of tickling had started inside the tip of his prick; he resisted the natural urge to touch himself, with some effort. Standing the way she was, on her high suede stilletto heels, she reminded him of something. A pin-up of the '40s. A Vargas girl, or the currently resurrected wartime photo of Betty Grable, the one prisoners of war used to wank over. (Or did the Red Cross humanely send out saltpetre to subdue the sex urge of all those poor devils?). It was the combination and contrast of the harsh slick line of the black satin suspender belt outlining the curve of her hips, and the frothiness of the white apron almost concealing it. The result was a graphic delight, though of course the girl inside helped. She exuded what was now an out-dated word, much in use in the era of those particular pin-ups; she exuded a great deal of 'oomph'.

But Randolph still felt that knickers were needed. 'A G-string. That's what you want with that outfit.' He put his head on one side. 'A black one with silky tassels at the crotch. You've got one of those, you used it on Easter Sunday when the kids went to All Saints Sunday School for tea. What were you — a Finnish stripper or something?'

Blossom spun round indignantly. 'A what? A Finnish stripper? I bloody well wasn't! I was a Mother Superior who by mistake had been sent some "erotic underwear to turn your

17

husband on" by a mail order firm. It was meant to be in the outer Hebrides; she'd sent for Thermal underwear for the harsh winter months. What on earth put Finland in your mind?'

'The weather conditions I expect.' Randolph rubbed his chin. 'Oh yes, I remember the Mother Superior. She was *very* good, you should do her again –'

Blossom sniffed huffily. 'It's not my practice to repeat myself – that's the whole point of the thing I should have thought, that you never have the same one again.'

'Your rule. Not mine. I actually do have some favourites that I would very much enjoy having again. It would make it much easier for you.'

Blossom crossed one long lissom leg over the other and laughed forgivingly. 'I rather enjoy the challenge,' she purred seductively. 'Shall I go now and put on my knickers . . .'

The Female Conference was very jolly, June found to her surprise. It was an invited audience of about 250 women, much larger than she had expected. And although there was a leading panel of ten on the platform there was a responsive participation from the rest of the hall. Individuals would freely stand and state their views, interruptions were welcomed, if not actively encouraged. The whole thing had a refreshingly lively feel to it, even the aggressively militant feminists were showing a rare sense of humour. One of them, a short, plump lady-wrestler with blonde hair and black roots had just made them all laugh a moment ago. She'd given an articulate account of how she had recently re-met the husband of years before, with whom she had led a miserable existence as a battered wife. Drunk and unaware of his ex-wife's new career he had made a vicious lunge at her in a Stepney pub. He was now residing in the Rehabilitation Wing of the hospital at Stoke Mandeville, a centre for the permanently disabled.

June was seated between a wry, witty barrister, who she suspected was gay, and a homely little woman with a wart on her nose who spoke with an incomprehensible Scottish accent. So incomprehensible was it that when she rose to her feet and spoke for fifteen minutes total silence ensued, which seemed to indicate that not a single person present had understood a word of what she had said. Until a fellow scotswoman at the back had given a rousing, 'Hear, hear!' followed by a positive storm of applause.

'My rough guess is that she was going on about North Sea oil,' whispered the witty barrister to June. 'I understand that she's a Member of Parliament, a Nationalist I shouldn't be surprised.'

June didn't speak because she was worried about time and was forced to leave in the middle of a most interesting paper, being read by a member of the panel on stage. The woman, a well-known gynaecologist, was explaining the revolutionary replacement of the womb in puberty in such a way as to banish menstruation and the menopause for good and all. She had already been enthusiastically questioned by an excited posse of expensively clad girls, who claimed matter-of-factly to be prostitutes. June would have liked to have heard more but had already cut it a bit fine for getting to the air terminal on time. The witty barrister passed her telephone number and whispered that she must get in touch, pressing her hand suggestively as she did so. June made her apologies to the rest of the row for having to make them stand and eventually made her escape.

Many people smiled at her on her way out, several mouthing 'hello'. They were all complete strangers who thought that they knew her simply because her face was familiar. It was becoming more familiar the busier she became. Only a year ago it would have been perfectly possible to walk around and lead her life in almost complete anonymity. The Late Show had had small and limited audiences, mainly intellectuals. But this situation was altering as her television appearances increased on the various channels; and, too, her recent programmes had had a far wider appeal. She was gradually becoming known to the public – whether she liked it or not.

Outside June tried hailing a taxi, to her relief one drew up immediately. The driver recognised her. 'I seen you on the telly,' he said pushily. 'Never forget a face. Now don't tell me – let me guess what it was you was on – it was with some old bloke talking about something. Was it Panorama? Or was it Nationwide? It was one of them sort of programmes, wasn't it – I know you, you're one of them brainy type of birds. All that women's lib sort of balls – now tell me if I'm right . . .' The conversation lasted one-sidedly all the way to the air terminal and for the first time June thought she detected a note of aggression directed at her — it wasn't a pleasant feeling. She caught a glimpse of what some of her better known colleagues had to put up with.

To her relief she found that she was the first to arrive. No one else had shown up, this suited her admirably. It gave her time to check how she looked in the Ladies. She had a small make-up bag, the one she took with her on these outside locations, and now was as good a time as any to adjust to a more exaggerated camera complexion. She began brushing a rich russet shadow beneath her clearly defined cheekbones, holding her head high to judge the effect from the harsh artificial lighting, turning her chin left and then right. The lavatory attendant was a swarthy, handsome Asian dressed in layers of screaming nylon garments, clashing lime with petunia, combining the ethnic harem trousers of the east with a mundane knitted cardigan of the west, in a drab fawn. She scowled with apparent loathing at June's friendly smile. And who could blame her, June thought, swabbing up and pulling chains all day long; her view of Great Britain was contained in this neon-lit landscape of porcelain wash-basins, liquid soap, rolled paper and lavatory bowls. The woman's smouldering eyes burned up the distance between them. She was mopping the floors of the furthest line of cubicles, using a large metal bucket and a long-handled mop for the job. Between each application of sudsy water, she slowly and methodically squeezed out the mop in the special fitment at the top of the pail, until it was dry enough to soak up more moisture. It seemed to June to be a uniquely dispiriting occupation and she was sure that the woman was doing it all wrong. According to the commercials she watched on the box, soapy suds were the old-fashioned way, taking twice as long to dry and leaving messy smears. Weren't sponges meant to be the thing now?

June was hazy about the actual practicalities of domesticity. She left that sort of thing to Blossom, a paragon of all those womanly virtues. But then Blossom loved her home, she cherished her possessions, her vast and colourful collection of china, of objets d'art, of odd furniture and exotic fittings. Blossom would not like or trust anyone other than herself to clean and take care of them. She delighted in her environment and was forever searching for further embellishments. June preferred to travel light. Even when she'd been with Tiny it had been his flat that they had shared and he was responsible for providing the cleaner. On the many occasions of their split-ups she had simply stayed with various friends. She had intended to find a place of her own all the time; but somehow it just hadn't happened. Finally she had ended up where she was now at Flowers, a small and cosy hotel around the corner from the Portobello Road – as a permanent guest. Permanent guests were *not* required to do housework.

June looked at her watch, the woman's gaze brought her back to reality. She felt suddenly self-conscious, keenly aware of the difference between their situations in life, and as she casually dropped the coin in the saucer placed for tips it seemed to add insult to injury. The final gesture in gracious condescension. She left, feeling relieved and it only occurred to her much later that she might well have been paranoiac. The simple reason for the woman's fierce attention was perhaps that she had merely seen June on television, and lacked the necessary vocabulary to communicate this. Her burning glances quite probably held no hostility at all, it was just that the sight of immigrants employed in inferior occupations always made June feel defensively guilty.

Stepping out into the lobby of the busy air terminal, concerned now that the airport coach was due to leave in five minutes and there was still no sign of either the crew or the director, June was startled to hear her name on the Tannoy. She hurried over to the reception desk and was told there was a message, an urgent call which they would transfer to one of the phone booths. It was the director in a state of panic, unusual even for him. Connor McConnors the Irish poet, was dead! Killed in an explosion on the outskirts of Dublin.

'A bomb!' June's brain raced.

'Apparently not. A domestic accident, a trivial thing, a faulty gas-stove that he'd hung onto for years. You know he lived in absolute squalor –' The director's high voice reached a new hysterical pitch. 'Wouldn't you just bloody credit it – I've been trying to pin this old bugger down long enough to get a programme on him for the past three sodding years, and then this has to happen! It means that the BBC has stolen a march on us again, the only television record in existence is that interview on Monitor – and that was done almost nineteen years ago –'

June remained silent. The man was steadily losing control.

21

She had seen him like this before. Though he had done some absolutely brilliant programmes, his sensitivity was now thought to be getting the better of him. He drank a lot when under pressure. June couldn't be certain but right now he seemed to have had a few. His words were slurring, and his reaction was becoming more emotional by the minute.

'So the schedule, I take it, is cancelled for today?' She spoke calmly as if completely unaffected by the tragic news or the last minute alteration to their plans. The crew were booked after all, it didn't necessarily mean that she wouldn't be working with them on something else.

'What's that?' The director was screaming now, tears were not far off. June was forced to hold the receiver some distance from her ear. She sighed softly, feeling suddenly weary. The events of last night and a hovering hangover were beginning to take their toll. She found herself praying that she wouldn't have to work this afternoon after all. It would be the first break that she would have had in weeks.

'I said—' she began.

'What's that?' The director was screaming again, but this time she felt that he was addressing someone else, the rest of the office presumably. 'Darling,' (now he was talking to her), 'could you just hang on half-a-mo? I'm just checking this end, it's bloody chaos here as you can imagine—we were planning to slot Connor McConnors in tomorrow night on the second half of Spectrum. Of course, if we'd done him last Friday as I had originally planned—remember you were working for the opposition that day down in Devon so I chose to postpone it till you were free—we would really have had a scoop. That's, of course, if the old bugger had still kicked the bucket today! With my luck he would have gone on forever—hey, hold on, someone has just walked in—.' June heard him screaming again. 'Jeremy, or any of you, I've got June Day here on the phone and a camera crew on call – does anybody want her?' June knew without listening what the response to that question would be. 'They all send you their best love, darling,' the director was back, 'but everything is just too disorganised this end – give me a number where we can get hold of you later. We may think of something live in the studio tomorrow – someone's shouting that Woody Allen's in town—.' June gave her agent's telephone number and gratefully left the terminal; it looked as if the rest of the day could be hers.

Randolph Tree lay on the kitchen floor near the sink, in a deeply satisfied post-coital sleep. He would lie there for quite some time if Blossom let him, and there was no reason why not for though his flies were wide open there was no fear of draughts. Randoph had to be careful of those; he was a person who caught colds all too easily.

Blossom eased herself off him, gently and with great care. Sometimes the faint 'plop' as his heavy prick emerged from her wet cunt (like a worm from the soil after a shower, she always thought) together with the soft thud as it slithered against his balls was enough to wake him. A shame. He claimed the post-coital slumber to be the best of all sleeps. So far today he had been privileged to enjoy four. Blossom was charging the rather ridiculous rate of a fiver a time, but then her charges had always been arbitrary. In any case Randolph had not been to the bank and it would have been wrong to accept a cheque. The sly and suggestive rustle of notes before the actual performance was all part of the erotic excitement. Indeed, such was the strong association now in her mind between paper money and sexual pleasure that sometimes in shops she'd found herself responding down below just queueing at the cash desk, whilst other housewives paid their bills. Randolph had been particularly interested when she had told him and had pressed her for further details, taking notes in the process. 'At which shops would you say this sensation was strongest? The butcher's, the baker's, the –'

'The candlestick maker's?' Blossom had added, not taking it seriously. But he had persisted, having recently re-read the famous tome by the eighteenth century philosopher, John Locke, *An Essay on Human Understanding* in which the principle of the association of ideas had been pursued. Blossom must think hard and speak honestly – her answers were vitally important, they might form the basis of serious research. They began again.

She had tried with some difficulty to be more specific. As she had pointed out, it wasn't so easy to say exactly *where* the quim had become activated. It might, in all truth, have actually started in the fish market. The marvellously pungent smell of fresh fish could have turned her thoughts in that direction without her realising it. Then again it may have been the warm, womb-like cave of the bakery, along with the phallic french loaves. Or for that matter, if symbolic shapes were going to enter (sic) into it, couldn't Freda's Fruiterer and Greengrocer come (sic) somewhere. (All the cucumbers and bananas, we must try all that again you know!)

Randolph had delightedly noted it all down, but had persisted until he had finally got her to admit that she first became conscious of actual wetness – indeed almost a sensation of *coming* near the cash counter of Liptons Supermarket in the High Street. Blossom was ashamed that it had taken place in such mundane surroundings, but there was nothing to be done about it. She knew from past dealings with Randolph that in matters of research absolute truth and scrupulous honesty were all-important.

Blossom knelt over the sleeping form and studied her husband's handsome face. 'God, but you're gorgeous,' she said fondly. A small tremor travelled over the sensual mouth, drawing the corners down derisively. Yet Blossom was certain that he couldn't have heard. She glanced down at her clothing, at her unbecoming nightdress and dreary woollen dressing-gown, purchased at a jumble sale in aid of the Lifeboat Appeal. A hair-curler had fallen from her head during the recent seduction scene (she had been playing the part of a frustrated housewife. Randolph was the shy and reluctant plumber, she'd had to use all her wiles to coax him onto the job). The curler had got caught up in the frayed cord of her dressing-gown, so that's what she'd been feeling all through!

Her knees fitted snugly each side of Randolph's hips. Earlier one knee had pinned him masterfully to the floor, despite his half-hearted struggle. She had approached him from behind as he'd bent to examine the plumbing, and had employed brute force to reduce him to the ground. He had given a frightened bleat of protest which she had chosen to ignore, and had mouthed half-formed sentences to register his alarm. She very much enjoyed his simulated panic. All in all it had been a highly successful session. She felt rather pleased with herself, but the question now was whether he would have the stamina to carry on.

She looked at the time (at the precise moment that June was consulting her watch at the air terminal). Randolph would be feeling like something to eat when he woke up. Screwing always gave him a tremendous appetite. Once, she remembered, he had consumed two entire meals in a restaurant they had driven to after bed. One after the other, just like that. The management had given them each a brandy on the house, and Randolph had ordered a further three so that they both got very drunk and behaved rather badly, doing a lot of shouting and passing rude comments about the people at other tables. But the management had still asked them graciously to come again. The bill had come to three times Blossom's weekly housekeeping allowance, but both of them agreed that it had been bloody worth it. In any case they had been celebrating, that day they had broken their own record. They had chalked up nine pokes in twelve hours, starting at six in the morning. One and a half times more than the previous time they'd tackled it, though they had been reluctant to admit that neither the eighth or the ninth were really worth having. Indeed poor Randolph had complained of actual physical pain at the point of so called orgasm. He'd said the sensation in his bollocks felt as if they were being internally shaved with a very sharp razor. He feared he might have done himself a permanent damage. Blossom suffered nothing other than a slight irritation when passing water, and perhaps a need to do this more often than usual. It was a condition that used to be referred to as Honeymoon Cunt when she was a student. She considered it rather chic to be able to boast of it after two children and twelve years of marriage!

Randolph stirred beneath her but didn't wake up. He looked tired, Blossom thought regretfully. It didn't seem as if they would be going for the elusive ten today. But she wouldn't like to think that at only nine fucks they had reached the peak of their performance. Nine was such an unremarkable sum. Ten sounded just that much more all-roundish. June thought so too, she was always asking, checking up to see if they had managed it yet. She didn't ask Randolph of course, Blossom hadn't ever told him that June knew anything about the record. She had an uneasy feeling that he might mind. Especially since he hadn't yet reached their perpetual goal. It irked him, any failure. And this he saw as a failure, a breakdown in the functioning between body and mind. But he had the wisdom never to have asked if Blossom had told June. He knew how it was between the two of them.

Blossom stood up, she felt stiff. The kitchen floor was hard, if she had thought about it she could have put cushions down. Although it would have been out of place in the erotic scenario. A frustrated housewife, after all, would hardly be likely to line her lair with goose feathers, and Blossom was very keen on a semblance of authenticity. Anyway, the kitchen floor was not the most uncomfortable working surface they had encountered. Not after they fucked in some of the bizarre locations that they had found.

She went over to the phone, which they always took off the hook when they were having a bit. Too often in the past they had suffered from untimely interruptions. Now Blossom returned the receiver to its hook. If Randolph had his way they wouldn't own a telephone at all. He considered it an unwelcome intrusion from the outside world. But Blossom had insisted, the telephone was her medium. She was a natural gossip and enjoyed the daily trading of tit-bits with all her friends. And in any case how else would she be able to talk to June? She thought of June now with a surge of feeling. She thought of how marvellous it would be to see her. Up until the children had been born she and June had always managed to spend at least several weeks of the year together. Either June had come down or else Blossom had gone to London. But that seemed somehow impossible to arrange any more. Though the children were certainly capable of taking care of themselves these days. This weekend they would be camping on the cliffs with their friends for two whole nights with not a single adult in sight, after all they were hardly babies now.

A pile of her clothing lay on the kitchen table, she'd had to change out of it in a hurry for this last one. Now she nimbly slipped out of her dressing-gown and drew the thick flannelette nightdress up over her head.

'Very nice.' Randolph was awake, sitting up with his knees apart and his cock hanging out of his jeans. It was difficult to think of him as being forty in a few months time. She must start planning what to get him for his birthday.

A button had got tangled with one of her hair-curlers, so that she was stuck with the nightdress high in the air over her stretched arms. Her head was half in and half out. 'Bloody hell

26

– can't you help me!' She wailed. Randolph remained where he was on the floor enjoying the view of his wife's wriggling torso. Although she had borne him two children, it would have been difficult to tell. Her body was as firm and as youthful as when they had first met. In her bikini on the beach several summers ago he had still found it impossible to tell the difference between her and June. But she took good care of herself physically.

'What time are we going swimming today?' he said conversationally. 'Have you consulted the tide chart yet?' His cock felt contentedly tender, studying it he could spot a fine, milky sheen drying already to invisibility in places. A combination of their accumulated juices.

'Sod swimming! Come and get me out of here!' Blossom's scarlet face bent down before him, peeping through the neck of her nightie.

'Do you need assistance? What seems to be the trouble?' Randolph ran boldly investigative hands between his wife's thighs, opening the slightly swollen flesh of her labia, and easing a gentle thumb inside.

'Christ! It's pouring wet in here!' he shouted. 'I shall catch a terrible cold – help me!'

Blossom struggled wildly, trying to back away. And squeezing her upper thighs closely together in an unsuccessful effort to shake his thumb out. 'You bastard!' she gasped. 'I shall – I shall, I shall *charge* you for this!!' She peered at him wildly through her restricting garment and her voice took on a note of rising triumph. 'There you are, you see, it's coming up – that'll be two pounds fifty for an incipient erection!'

June had a late lunch with her agent in Soho, around the corner from the office, which was in a small mews off Berwick Market. June had called in to check whether she'd be needed this afternoon or not.

'The answer to that, my darling, is "Non". Ah but – you wait for it – they are wanting you tomorrow at nine-thirty for a studio interview with a surprise guest on Spectrum. Is very, very good for you, little one, I think. That surprise guest is no other than Dame Tiger Oats! Is she not the famous relic of the twenties, yes? That naughty boy, Zachary Ram, 'e say to me on the line that with luck she will expire on the programme! I 'ave the belief that they are doing it live.'

Cherie Pye, June's clever agent, was an exquisite Parisienne who had trained as a ballerina when a child. She was tiny and intense, with large brown eyes and a small compressed mouth. Her coal-black hair fell as far as her waist when she combed it out, but she wore it coiled like a serpent at the nape of her neck during the day, and in the evening piled it on the top of her head like a plate of profiteroles. Only at night in bed was it allowed to hang loose. She had been married three times, was separated from Samson Pye, her present husband, although she talked incessantly of a possible reconciliation. She had endured two heart-breaking miscarriages following four flippant abortions and had been medically advised never to attempt another pregnancy ever again. She was obsessed with small babies, Samson Pye, her clients' careers, casual sexual encounters with unusual partners, and above all she was obsessed with her weight. She smoked and coughed continuously and suffered intermittently from *anorexia nervosa*, having twice brought herself to the brink of death through self-induced starvation.

But despite her (or perhaps because of her) neuroses she was an inspired agent, who pursued her clients' interests with the persistence of a maggot. She had been one of the most highly respected members of her profession, at a time when female agents were relatively few and far between. Her skills were considered to be legendary. June was keenly aware of how very fortunate she was to be with Cherie Pye, but her professional regard didn't interfere with the affection the two felt for each other. Despite the distance of years they had a great rapport; there was some fifteen years between them, but Cherie was a sophisticated and sensual forty-five with a basic and black sense of humour. Her sheer style appealed to June enormously, she had always thought that was how she would like to be at that age – without the neuroses of course, and all the personal dramas, but then that was simply all part of the Gallic high temperament.

They sat side by side, on show, at Chez Stalky. Cherie insisted on doing so whenever they ate there, so that not only would they both be in a fine position to see who was in the rest of the restaurant, but that the rest of the restaurant should see them.

Stalky, the smiling proprietor, was delighted to welcome them. He manoeuvred his substantial paunch between the occupied chairs in an attempt to greet them as soon as they came in. June suspected that he had always been more than a little in love with Cherie (as was everyone – just a little bit). But no one would have known, his welcoming embrace was equally warm for each of them. 'My two favourite girlfriends!' Heads swivelled. Stalky's thick Glaswegian accent cut through the cultured discourse of chattering diners. June suspected that the reason Cherie always chose to take her to Stalky's was that he enabled her to effect this dramatic entrance. But they did look a stunning pair. Cherie was wearing a silver kid trouser suit more appropriate to a teeny-bopper rock star than a woman of maturing years. Yet on her it seemed to be the height of absolute chic, outrageously alluring, each movement attracting the change of light to its shining surface. Accentuating the extreme slenderness of her small, tight body, so that the gleaming silver appeared to have been sprayed on.

Following this dazzling apparition into the restaurant June couldn't resist a delighted smile. Her position afforded her a view of Cherie's straight triangular back in its short bomber jacket slicked into the waist – 'bum-freezers' they were known in the rag-trade. And they certainly placed the bum on display. June found herself mesmerized by the sinuous roll of Cherie's boyish buttocks before her, so temptingly pinchable. She was sure that Blossom had a gold suit similar to this one, or had at one time around the middle of the '60's. She must have done, Blossom's wardrobe was absolutely amazing; there wasn't any style or period that she hadn't owned since she'd been married to Randolph. June envied her that – Tiny had always frowned on any tendency towards flamboyance. And since then she had stayed on the side of sartorial reserve. But Cherie approved.

'June darling, you are looking – 'ow do we say – absolument in the pink! I like very much what you 'ave on your back today. Is fabulous, that shit colour so close to your face. Tell me what is the place you 'ave bought this dress – I must consider something drab like that for me. Is time, do you not agree, that I start to dress suitable to my position in life? But you know, I spotted this silver suit in a children's boutique on the Kings Road and I simply could not resist it – and the fit, is *merveilleuse, non*!' Cherie sighed and rolled her eyes, patting her flat belly. 'Oh, but I am getting *so* fat! Yes, but I am – don't I know it –'

June frowned at her. 'Don't start all that, for Christ's sake, or I shall walk out right now.'

Cherie coughed protestingly over her freshly lit cigarette, then took another drag, preparing to speak in her own defence. But June beat her to it. 'We are not discussing it today, all right? We both know perfectly well that your end will be brought about by lung cancer and not obesity, and pretty soon by the sound of that cough, Cherie. Have you seen to it lately? It's like being with a barking dog!' June was enjoying herself. She did when admonishing heavy smokers. Having given up the habit over two years ago, and not succumbed since to the ever present temptation, she felt the zealous scorn of the smugly converted. Though there was an element of self-protection in her sanctimonious attack, the strong desire for a cigarette still lurked in her system, surfacing unexpectedly at times like these, in seductive surroundings with a glass of wine in the hand and the spaces between words waiting to be filled. Not that there was much waiting between words with Cherie.

'*Mon dieu*! You are so, so stern today – you are a miserable bitch! Tell me,' the throaty accent splintered from a stifled cough into a suggestive chuckle, 'what you were up to last night, little one, to place you in this disagreeable frame of mind? I tell you – I 'ave the answer. Stalky!' She summoned him shrilly. 'Stalky! You must come and choose from the menu – my adorable June 'ere is in a bad mood. I think, yes, that she 'as the constipation – you must give her something very kind to open her poor bowels . . .'

By the middle of the lunch June felt pleasantly airborne, but she knew from experience that this was the danger point. Cherie was gaiety itself and had gathered the best of the rest of the restaurant around their table, crashing into the brandy. Her manner of invitation was nothing if not imperious. Since she and June had arrived so late, many tables were already preparing to empty at the time of their spectacular entry. Several lingered out of a mixture of professional interest, natural curiosity and undisguised lust. Chez Stalky was, at lunchtimes, frequented primarily by men. Cherie, well aware of the longing glances being levelled at their much cherished table (much cherished because it was permanently vacant in the corner, reserved by Stalky for his special favourites), had made her choice as to whom should be allowed to sit with them. At the moment of decision, following shamelessly brazen scrutiny of the scene, she would snap her fingers in the direction of the eager victim and graciously incline her handsome head. June, regarding the tilt of the long and vulnerable neck, thought how smashing the teen Cherie must have been tip-toeing about in *Swan Lake*. June noticed she had barely eaten a thing. The artichoke she had chosen to start with had eventually been borne away still practically intact. June could guess at the reaction in the kitchen: 'Just look at this sodding artichoke, some joker's been picking away at one or two of these outer leaves! Making sure we can't offer it out again!' And her rare fillet steak lay untouched on its wooden plate, gently leaking a thin trickle of watery blood from a half-hearted attack some time before, when Cherie had actually seemed about to consume something because her fork had made contact with the meat. But then nice Nobs Plater (everyone's favourite newscaster) and Zachary Ram, the mischievous television critic of the weekly magazine *Views*, had presented themselves at the table. There was no eating anything after that. June rather regretted the way that their intimate lunch had escalated into of such a high-powered salon. She had been looking forward to relating her misdeeds of the previous night. So far she hadn't had the fun of telling anyone about the Director General. She'd tried Blossom but the line seemed to have been permanently engaged. She knew what that meant – they were obviously on the job, with the phone off the hook. That was why she had actually called into Cherie's office, to see her face and her sly reaction to this latest piece of gossip. She and her agent shared all their sexual secrets.

There was a slight lull in the proceedings, a noted man of letters had just joined the proprietorial inner group closest to Cherie and June. His name was Professor Hamilton Hamilton and although June had seen him many times on the box, and passed him, his scholarly head high in the clouds, along the corridors of Television Tower on the way to the studio, she had never met him before. And yet, repeatedly, he was smiling at her and nodding his head as if in recognition; June could only conclude that because he must have also seen her on the small screen, he genuinely felt that he knew her. And so she smiled back. Of course he was an intimate of Cherie's. ' 'am-'am, mon cheri!' She had cried on sight, waving both dazzling silver arms in the air. But it had been June to whom his warm and humorous gaze returned, until even Cherie began to notice. She made use of the lull to mention the fact. 'Darling? You 'ave to tell me, *non*, what you think of 'am-'am, as a lover! 'E is a sexy old goat now, but can you believe that I 'ad 'im first time for me as a student at the Sorbonne. 'E was not a professor in those days – far from it. But 'e 'ad a most knowledgeable penis. Now tell me is 'e that man that you were 'aving last night?' Her eyes shone with anticipation.

June shook her head swiftly. 'Believe it or not I don't even know the good Professor Hamilton Hamilton, but,' she lowered her voice, aware that Zachary Ram on her right could play certain havoc with the piece of juicy gossip she was about to impart, 'the person I landed in bed with, believe it or not, was . . . she paused for greater effect and to relish for a moment longer the expression on Cherie's face, 'the person was the Director General of Universal Television himself!' And she sat back to savour her agent's reaction.

It was not the reaction she had expected.

Cherie went white and immediately started eating without stopping. Within moments she had not only demolished her cold, congealed steak, but had ripped two bread rolls into pieces and was busy wolfing them down, whilst viciously shredding at an inoffensive stick of celery and looking wildly round the littered table for something else to get her teeth into. June stared at her with amazement and mounting alarm.

'Jesus!' she whispered. 'Is he one of yours!' Christ – she knew it would be bound to bloody happen one day! Yet up until now their taste in men had never overlapped, which was probably one of the reasons they got on so well. She tried to conjure up what picture she could of the Director General. Of course it wasn't fair to judge a person's appearance and sex appeal, not when they are suffering the distorting spasms of an imminent seizure, or even when (as this morning, thankfully) that person then emerges from near tragedy in a miraculous recovery. But even so June would never have thought that the Director General was Cherie's type. But he obviously was, otherwise why on earth this extraordinary reaction! June could kick herself for the error, but she could see now that perhaps Cherie had at last grown tired of her procession of handsome men and beautiful boys. Samson Pye her beloved, absent, husband wasn't beautiful after all, and certainly not young. In fact the more June thought about it, Samson Pye was in many ways not unlike the Director General – a substantial and influential figure of authority. And June would have been the last to deny the sexual potency of power – wasn't that precisely what she had succumbed to last night? She glanced around discreetly. The bloody fat could be in the fire if Cherie were to have a momentary aberration and spill the beans at this gathering. She had already spilt nice Nobs Plater's large brandy, without his noticing, in a frenzied attempt to reach the leftover Marrons Glacés on the next table. But there appeared to be one of those intellectual discussions of high intent in progress, one about to deteriorate into a free-for-all debate before ending in actual argument. The only person whose eye she did catch was the watchful Professor. She made the point of again exchanging a sweet smile.

It must have been just what he wanted, just what he had been waiting for, the final encouragement.

'Would you mind awfully, old chap,' he leant towards Zachary Ram, 'if I were to ask you to change places with me? In my opinion you have been in the hot seat for too long – only fair to allow somebody else a fair crack of the whip – eh?' Within seconds he was seated at June's side.

Cherie was deep in conversation with a gratified Stalky trying to decide between Crêpes Suzettes on the vast menu, or Soufflé au Grand Marnier. Since the flavour of both would be virtually indistinguishable their discussion was based on the difference in texture. This was a great occasion for Stalky, in all the years that Cherie had eaten at his emporium this was the first time that he had known her show interest in afters. And he was very much a pudding-person himself; though he would have preferred to tempt her to something more original than the choice in question, he didn't dare start rocking the boat now. June sat in dubious silence listening to their animated discourse. She had only once before witnessed Cherie in this manic tuck-munching mood, and that was when the estranged Samson Pye had, at the very last minute, cancelled their plans for a dirty weekend in a place called Worms, near Frankfurt in West Germany. Cherie had been so looking forward to sending back postcards from Worms. But after the eating bout she had spent the next half-hour in the lavatory forcing her fingers to the back of her throat until the entire bumper meal had been vomited away. June felt that old Stalky's delicious dessert would eventually suffer the same shabby fate.

But now Professor Hamilton Hamilton was pressing her hand to his lips and his twinkling eyes were crinkling away like mad at her own. Something lurched in her stomach, a thread of sexual excitement. It was solely to do with the eminence of the man, a repeat of last night, all over again – she was being pulled by the palpable power. And the challenge of course.

'Well, well,' he was whispering with an unaccountable familiarity. June simpered, aware of curious eyes upon them. Professor Hamilton Hamilton had enjoyed the reputation of being a dedicated ladies' man. His choice in the past, before the death of his wife, had always veered between females of distinction. There had been the series of scandalous affairs with well-known women; the articulate wife of the American Ambassador; the svelte singing star of a long-running musical; the fey French novelist who had finally committed suicide in her suite at the Savoy, because he had steadfastly refused to leave his wife. And then his wife had left him, dying of cancer within three weeks of its diagnosis. He was shattered. Some said she was getting her own back.

But since her death he had maintained a very low profile, his illustrious name had been linked with no one at all. (Might June Day prove the exception? That's what the rest of the table were wondering.) He was still holding her hand, he hadn't let it go. June looked down at their lightly laced fingers and inwardly shivered. She was a remarkably attractive girl, she knew that if only by looking at Blossom, but this effortless conquest had taken her by surprise. It wasn't always as *instant* as this.

She cleared her throat self-consciously, having been about to enquire rather pompously whether or not they had actually been introduced in the past. She could, in all honesty, never be positively sure whether she had met strangers before – or even have been to bed with them for that matter. At the arse-holed end of many evenings she was certain that she'd staggered off with many a choice mortal who she'd be hard put to recognise by the cold light of morning. It happened to anyone with half an ounce of oomph – didn't it?

But Professor Hamilton Hamilton had beaten her to it. 'Well, well,' he was murmuring, 'and so we meet again!'

That was it then. June smiled slowly as if reliving the pleasant memory of their meeting. The thing was to coast now, box clever, just picking up clues as to where that meeting may have taken place. But she needn't have bothered – no coasting, no boxing clever, no picking up clues – they were all quite unnecessary. Professor Hamilton Hamilton's following words made that perfectly clear. 'Blossom. Enchanting Blossom – my loving thoughts have never left you . . .'

The pounding blood in her brain deafened June's ears to the rest of the sentence. It was twelve years since the last time this sort of thing had happened; and two weeks later that man had become her brother-in-law! But she hadn't time to ponder on that sweet memory, although her brother-in-law's name had already insinuated itself into the conversation.

'. . . and Randolph – how is the dear chap? I wish we could winkle him away from your splendid Cornish retreat sometime. Only last month his name cropped up at Disciple's Dinner for this year's Hector Fellowship. He's been awarded it several times before and each time he has refused the honour – do you think that he will turn down the Global Prize?'

'The Global Prize!' June knew that Randy (she and Blossom were the only two in the world allowed to call him Randy) divulged little of what he deemed unimportant to Blossom. Did he then consider the Global Prize to be of no value? He must do, since Blossom had not mentioned the smallest thing about it, and if she had known anything – even had she been sworn to utter secrecy – then June would have been put in the picture. 'For *Understanding Understanding*. In my opinion it is the most brilliant paper of its kind – and the genius of the man to have written it all in Babylonian.' Professor Hamilton Hamilton permitted himself a sly, but modest smile. 'Of course I was one of the few in this country who had no reason to wait for the tardy official translation – I read Babylonian as if it were the Beano comic . . .'

June's thoughts raced back to the previous Easter, to the time when Blossom had tried to persuade her to take a break and come down. She remembered that Randy had been cloistered up in his study for months.

'For God's sake do come down – I'm going mad with him,

35

June! He only emerges for a fuck and some food, and he's bab-
bling away in what he claims to be Babylonian – he even answers the phone with it. People are surprised when they see me
out shopping in the streets. The rumour was going around that
we had let the house to Arabs!'

The obtuse *Understanding Understanding* (a typical Randolph
Tree title) was obviously the outcome of that time. But when
would Blossom and the Professor have met? June racked her
brains for the answer to that. She could only assume that it
must have been when she and Tiny had gone on their walking
holiday in Snowdonia in a last bid to resolve the difficulties between them. His idea, not hers, she had hated having to hike
about with a heavy rucksack concertina-ing her spinal column.
Shoulders back, breasts flung forward like the proud prow of a
sea-going vessel. It had rained heavily the entire time and her
shoes had developed a dispiriting leak. She had missed Blossom
dreadfully, Tiny's circuitous route had not allowed for casual
telephone conversations. When she returned, a week sooner
than intended – leaving Tiny on the water-sodden banks of the
River Usk, she and Blossom had spent all of two hours on the
phone. But it was still possible that Blossom had forgotten to
make mention of the frisky Professor.

One thing was quite certain. The relationship between them
had not been as intimate as Professor Hamilton Hamilton
would have liked. Blossom, though fencing flirtatiously with
her many fanciers, would never have been unfaithful to Randy.
Fidelity was one of the absolute rules of their marriage, one of
the sound principles of its trusting success.

But the time had come to disclose the crucial information
that she was not in fact Blossom.

'Professor – I'm not Blossom.' The Professor's bony knee was
busy nudging her own, not unpleasantly. As he smiled his wide
mouth revealed quite a decent set of teeth for a man of his age,
though of course he had always been a much-quoted veg-
etarian. June supposed that all those carrots must have kept
them going. She felt a bit of a pang, wondering whether, now
she turned out to be someone other than Blossom Tree, he
would stop ogling her altogether. It could happen. Being Blossom meant being not a simply highly desirable woman, but
being the wife of *the* Randolph Tree. An impressive entity to a
man of mind such as the Professor. More than once she herself

had deliberately engaged the attention of attractive and scholarly men, who until then had shown no interest in her whatsoever, by letting them know that she was the sister-in-law of Randolph Tree. Not only that, but the *twin* sister-in-law . . . Lying in bed later it amused her to know that they were as excited by this knowledge as they were by her body. That they held in their arms the facsimile of that which Randolph Tree held in his, just as if they were worshiping the very same woman.

A sudden slurping sound to the left of her distracted her attention momentarily. June turned at the noise. Stalky and Cherie were sampling their choices and swilling it all down with champagne, that was all.

Since the sexual revelation over the Director General, Cherie and June had not exchanged a single word. But now, seeing June's face, Cherie took the opportunity to nod vigorously with her mouthful. She also gave a very knowing, lewd wink and jerked her free thumb in the direction of the Professor. June was relieved that Cherie appeared to harbour no undue resentment over last night at least. And probably, knowing the volatile and sometimes completely irrational nature of her agent, she might never learn the reason for her unexpected reaction. Now was certainly not the moment to pursue the matter anyhow. June turned her attention back to Professor Hamilton Hamilton.

To her intense disappointment he was preparing to leave. He was signalling a passing waiter and wishing to settle his share of the brandy bottle on the table. He leaned towards June. 'I am so very, very sorry, charming girl – I fear that I have made a ridiculous figure of myself. But you are the image of a ravishing creature I once fell in love with, for a moment I completely forgot myself . . .'

June stared at him. In a moment she was about to lose a man whose name was a household word in this country. Whose writings were read all over the world. Whose reputation would go down in history. She could imagine the fun she'd be able to have with Blossom on the phone, the kudos with colleagues at work, the salacious comparison of notes with Cherie if she managed to pull this one into the net. Also wouldn't it mean that within less than twenty-four hours she would have fried two of the biggest fish in the London pool! She blinked her eyes several times to bring a brighter sheen to their brilliant colour. She licked her lips and drew them back to display her white and perfectly even teeth. She tossed her flaming hair over the slender curve of her shoulder.

And then she went in for the kill.

High tide was due at 16.55, which gave Blossom a good chance to do her weekend shopping first, or at least part of it. She very much enjoyed popping into the shops, seeing who she could see, swapping gossip and chatting. Sometimes she managed to trot out as often as three times in the same afternoon for some culinary item or other. 'I'm back!' She'd laugh gaily, darting into The Stores, Puddlemouth's old-fashioned grocery and off-licence. 'Well, I'll be blessed if she's not back again!' 'She's never back again . . .' 'She is that!' And the genial trio of apple-cheeked Cornish crones behind the counter would chuckle and shake their heads, each covered by the latest beret they'd just crocheted with the Women's Institute to match up with the nicely home-knitted cardigans. 'One day, my girl, you'll go forgettin' your 'ead!' 'That she will, that she will, that she will!'

Blossom loved it, the attention. She would squirm and dimple like a small child basking in the affectionate admonition of favourite aunties. 'It's as warm as the womb in there,' she had once confided to Randolph on her return. 'Do you suppose that is why I feel the need to keep returning?'

'What – a womb without June?' he had answered mockingly. 'You would find that a trifle draughty.'

'You pompous prick. You always take what I say so – so fucking literally.' It was early April and the weather had been glorious for a week, but today it was drizzling. Blossom hoped for the kids' sake that it would clear up for tomorrow, though she knew that even a torrential downpour wouldn't put them off camping now they had decided upon it. 'I'm off out to The Stores,' she shouted up the stairs wondering whether she should have put her rubber mackintosh on before, or after, doing so. With luck Randolph wouldn't have noticed it was raining. If however he had, then he would probably at this precise second be putting two and two together. In which case Blossom could expect him to come pounding down the stairs in a matter of moments. He had never been able to resist the thought of her in her rubber mackintosh.

That would mean a further delay of fifteen minutes!

She hadn't that much time to spare. There was a Jumble Sale in the Chapel, run by Emily Shawl, in aid of the forthcoming Easter outing to Seal Island for the under-fives, and another, scheduled for tomorrow morning, with the Salvation Army. But Blossom, along with the chosen few, had been invited to this afternoon's preview at the Sally Army. Last time their Jumble had yielded a bumper crop of old pinafores, the wrap-around kind, in sprigged William Morris prints. The sort that Libertys would have given their eye-teeth for. The son of Cuthbert and Son, Ironmongery and Haberdashery, a man in his late seventies had discovered the pinafores at the back of his stockroom. He still played the drums for the Salvation Army. Randolph had reason to curse him horribly every Sunday morning when the pious and uniformed holy regiment gathered beneath the bedroom window to blast out their hymns of praise. Sunday morning was the one morning that Randolph had a nice lie-in, it was his only acknowledgement to the official day of rest.

Blossom held her breath. There was no sound at all from upstairs. She was wondering whether Randolph had perhaps taken advantage of this brief respite before swimming to snatch another forty winks. His post-coitals were all very well in their place, but in her opinion they didn't count as real rest, whatever he said. And at lunch, late though it was, she felt that he was looking somewhat weary. And indeed had remarked upon it. 'You look positively *haggard*, my darling.' She had honestly meant it kindly. She herself felt and looked the opposite as he was quick to point out.

'Yes, well, there's nothing to be done about that – it's the physiological difference between the female and male species–'

She held up her hand with an offensively radiant smile as he was about to reply. 'No, my angel, I don't want to go into it now.'

But a little later, when he tried to stand up and she saw him actually *buckle* at the knees, then she was sorry that she had spoken so briskly.

There was still no sound from his study. Blossom stealthily slid into her rubbery covering. 'Black as death, but as shiny as sin', that's how he had described it when she had first brought the mac home.

39

'Is sin shiny?' She had been in the mood for a discussion that day.

'It's inviting.'

'That's not the same.'

'Association of ideas — something shiny to a child, to a magpie, that sort of thing . . .'

'I think it should be "black as death, but as shiny as . . ."'

'Spring?' Randolph had smiled. He was keen on spring, he was always grateful that the girls had been born in June and therefore christened that way (June and Blossom to avoid confusion between the two as to which of them was the elder, albeit by a mere twenty minutes). Their names were a continuing reminder to him of his favourite season. Blossom had laughed, she was enjoying herself. She loved the effrontery of pitting her inferior vocabulary against Randolph's. What she appreciated was that he never condescended to her in any way, as a more stupid man may have done. But then he never had. It was one of the many qualities for which she loved him so much.

'I love you,' she had said impulsively.

It was his turn to laugh. 'What about "spring"?' He was very, very stubborn, as well as everything else, but even managed to turn that into an endearing trait in Blossom's eyes.

'Every man likes the smell of his own farts.' She'd changed the subject.

'What has that to do with spring?'

'It's an Icelandic proverb — I found it in your book of aphorisms.'

'So?'

Blossom had kissed him slowly, running her tongue suggestively along the moist rim of his full upper lip, then insinuating the tip of it in between his half-open mouth. 'Black as death, but as shiny as sex — how about that?' she had murmured, unzipping his trousers. Then she had masturbated him daintily with the tips of her fingers (playing the part of a Victorian virgin), until he had shot off all down the front of the brand new mackintosh, clogging up three of the button-holes. It was interesting to note how copiously he had come.

The Salvation Army Jumble was somewhat of a disappointment. Except for one thing — a magnificent collapsible opera hat which when packed lay flat as a plate in its crimson cardboard box, but when banged sharply against the thigh sprang immediately into a grandiose shape. Everyone burst into cackles of glee when Blossom placed it on her head.

'What do you think then?' She tipped it at a more rakish angle.

'S'beautiful, my 'andsome!' 'Aye, aye, 'tis that – you goin' t'wear it at yer own funeral, are yer now!' Young Mrs Tree, though a foreigner – not coming from Cornwall at all, was nevertheless very popular with the locals. She was known as being a bit of a card, and the sort who could take a bit of a leg-pull. Of course her husband was a very clever fellow with his books and suchlike, but young Mrs Tree was the one who got on with everyone. And she was one of twins which turned her into the object of superstitious gossip, added to which she assumed the glamour of reflected glory from the fact of June becoming established as a television personality. 'C'm'ere quick, there is our young Missus Tree on the telly!' 'No, t'aint 'er, 'tis 'er twin. Them's alike as two peas in a pod.' 'Well, I never did – I could've sworn 'twas 'er!' The exchange was a common occurrence.

Blossom bought the opera hat, paying a pound for it to make up for the fact that she hadn't been tempted by anything else. The rest was the usual paraphernalia of matted woollies and garments moth-eaten beyond description, all smelling sourly of mildew. There was one positively hideous crimplene evening dress in a depressing dusty pink, with a raised surface like that of a person suffering from acne. Blossom toyed with it in her mind, as a possible if ever she thought of playing the part of a very plain wall-flower. But she was put off by the heavy under-arm stains, and knew that Randolph would most certainly have been revolted by them too (though of course that would have been all part of the exercise!) Picking her way carefully over the slippery, wet cobbles of Puddlemouth's many narrow alleyways and back passages Blossom looked forward to Emily Shawl's Chapel Jumble as being somewhat superior.

She kept her eyes widely on the ground, it wouldn't do to look up for an instant! Not with the surface of the streets so bespoiled with this much dog-shit! The canine deposits, their abundance and the haphazard manner of their placing, were the continuing disgrace of the otherwise picturesque Puddlemouth. The hordes of summer visitors who descended in the season expressed horror each year at this blatant disregard of hygiene, unaware that the situation in the summer was rather an improvement on the rest of the year. In the summer many of the turds were deposited on the sands, whilst proud and sauntering pet-owners cooed their congratulations. The hazards to packed lunches and picnic spreads, to bare toes and crawling babies, and the scores of half-naked spread-eagled on the beaches, were immeasurably greater. And Emily Shawl was the leading force in the local Anti Dog Shit Campaign. Her very next Jumble was to be held in aid of funds for the recently formed ADSC. They planned to take an entire page to publish all the names on their petition in the local newspaper, the *Puddlemouth Weekly*. The names of Blossom and Randolph Tree were there on the petition rather towards the end since it was listed alphabetically; in fact they had been amongst the very first to sign.

It would have been difficult to have withheld their signature from Emily Shawl, even if their support had not been wholeheartedly behind the scheme. Emily Shawl was a law unto herself, the self-appointed organiser of causes, with enough natural enthusiasm to carry a whole army. 'If 'n them Germans 'ad 'ad Emily Shawl on their side we'd 'ave lost the last bloody war – aye, without shadow of doubt!' This was the general opinion. A generous friend but a dangerous enemy. But she and Blossom had always got on.

'Howdy!' Emily's upper class consonants carried clear through the confusion of harrassed bargain hunters in the large Chapel vestry. She had been to RADA, a very long time ago, and still remembered how to throw her voice.

Blossom waved, she was dripping wet and thought about her imminent swim with an inward shudder. But she would do it, of course, and probably enjoy it immensely. Randolph never let a little thing like a simple shower put him off – not when they went in during the winter, even when there was snow on the ground. Being wet all over was much nicer than this damp which was seeping down the back of her neck and up her sleeves, and inside her ankle boots.

'Bitch of a day!' Emily's large and handsome profile swivelled sharply to her left as an avid forager pounced at the bundle of clothing beneath Emily's strong arm. 'Sorry, ducky – these are all spoken for –' She rapped the eager woman's grasping hand and, heedless of the resulting whimper of pain, strode over

42

towards Blossom at the door.

'Managed to save these for you, Blossom – thought they were rather your sort of thing.'

Blossom gasped her appreciation. 'Oh, Em, you are sweet!' It was a continuing source of embarrassment to Blossom that she couldn't be certain (she'd been very drunk at the time), but she *thought* that one New Year's Eve she had confided in Emily. She had told her all about her fantasy roles with Randolph and how much of a stimulus it was to their sex life. It had come out of discussing Emily's days at RADA and her failed career as an actress. Blossom supposed that she must have been after some thespian tips since she was on-stage for Randolph certainly twice-nightly. With a good chance of a matinée most days. She couldn't be *sure*, but she felt there to be an image stamped on her retina of Emily Shawl's high surprised pencilled eyebrows and her heavily rouged powdered cheeks all bunched together in an expression of camp outrage. The image was memorable because even at the time it had so reminded Blossom of a painting or coloured drawing she had seen of poor Oscar Wilde before his spirit had been broken. Since then she hadn't been able to see the swooping and posturing Emily without connecting the two together.

'How's Pots?' Blossom enquired solicitously, whilst sorting through the clothes. 'Is her cold any better – I haven't seen her for days.' Pots was Emily Shawl's friend and protegé, a pale and sickly young unmarried mother whose baby had just died when they had first come into contact with each other. It was Emily who had revived Pots from her overdose of sleeping tablets, bringing her down to Puddlemouth to live, caring for her with all the devotion of the dedicated, and coaxing some frail interest in life from that barely flickering spirit. Until the gradual metamorphosis had come about. Seeing Pots now, a relatively confident person and qualified infant-school teacher (Emily had financed her further education), it was difficult to believe she was the same creature. True, there was about her a timidity and certain shyness but in her job amongst the tiniest children these qualities were seen to be an advantage. It simply meant that this gentle soul shared the vulnerability of her charges which led to a greater understanding between them. They lived together, Emily and Pots, in The Mermaid's Nest. Emily's thriving Bed and Breakfast business was one of the few of its

4

sort which actually kept open all the year round. Most of them simply operated in the season, between Easter until the end of September. October if the weather held out. Then the small B&B signs would be withdrawn from the windows just as the cafés, the novelty shops, the Amusement Arcade, the Go-Go Boutique and the ice-cream parlour along the sea-front were being shuttered and locked till the following season.

But The Mermaid's Nest wasn't Emily Shawl's sole occupation. Her redoubtable fund of energy would not have been satisfied to be only spent on that. She was also the highly efficient curator of The Puddlemouth Society of Artists, (not affiliated in any way with the now largely extinct Puddlemouth Royal Academy of Artists) who had at their inception prided themselves on their modernity and vowed to adhere to their catholic principles. In the cause of Art, all is allowable.

And so it was. For many years freedom of expression reigned supreme – until in the mid-sixties it ran riot.

For one internationally famed fortnight the Puddlemouth Society of Artists became a cultural mecca for the avant-garde. The media descended. The town-councillors convened. A mixed group of multi-racial students marched nude through the cobbled streets in political protest, culminating in a sexual orgy on the sands in which many of the locals were pleased to participate. *The News of the World* carried it for two issues as its centre spread. Blossom and June, who were only fifteen at the time, were considering running away from home in order to join in. Randolph was there already, it was how he had first become accquainted with Puddlemouth.

And then suddenly it was all over, as if it had never been.

The Puddlemouth Society of Artists had revelled in their hour of glory. For a brief moment they had relished the fame – as had the locals, once they had grown used to being photo-graphed registering mock-horror and disgust. And for some time after there lingered a pronounced sense of anti-climax. But even this proved to be a unifying force consolidating the warmth of the communtiy. Conversations could still be heard between the folk who had lived through those hectic weeks. For some it seemed as if it had only happened yesterday. Emily Shawl had arrived in Puddlemouth at just the right moment to restore a sense of order to the Society of Artists.

'Pots?' she said now, her expression softening. 'Poor little

Pots. I have made her stay in bed all this week. Which reminds me – I shall have to go soon and give her some tea. Would you like some? You're very welcome, I made scones this morning. And it's my own strawberry jam from last summer.'

Blossom laughed. 'Sounds delish, but I can't. We're due to go swimming when I get back and I still haven't been to The Stores yet. These things are perfect by the way –' She held up a pair of thick corduroy jodhpurs and a gentleman's morning suit, the jacket complete with tails. Emily knew perfectly well that Blossom never went riding; and the gent's clothing was quite obviously far too small for Randolph. Emily winked. 'I thought they might come in handy for you know what.'

The sea was tumultous, it was impossible to swim. All Blossom and Randolph could do was stand at the edge and splash around in the surf. More than once Blossom got knocked off her feet by the force of the massive waves and even Randolph lost his balance several times. They clung together, laughing helplessly like children.

'The kids would love this –' Blossom shouted above the roar of the ocean.

'Who?' Randolph yelled back.

'The kids –'

'Oh, bugger the kids.' Randolph tightened his grip around her waist. 'I like it without them, don't you?' The wind carried his words off over the cliffs. Blossom hoped in a motherly way that Willow and Pip wouldn't hear, although they were a good twenty-five miles in the other direction. It was only recently that she had begun to feel vaguely guilty about the children in this way. Realising with a pang that she hadn't given them a single thought for hours at an end when they were out at school all day or when they were away. She supposed that it was all part of the gradual process of them growing up and away from herself as a parent, forging their independence and all that sort of thing. And yet it seemed to have happened so quickly. Only yesterday she was changing their nappies and powdering their botties, worrying about them every minute of the day. And waking in the night at the slightest murmur from their cots, mindful of the smallest sign of distress. She was a good mother, she knew that, but it was just that lately she was becoming increasingly aware of her diminishing involvement. She must remember to talk about it to June.

'Have we had enough then?' Randolph was shouting. A fresh avalanche of spray foamed and bubbled around their bodies, an icy inferno. They were the only ones in the water, except for several rubber-suited surfers waiting some distance out for the perfect wave to break. It wouldn't come today, the conditions were bad. These must be inexperienced surfers otherwise they would know that and give up. Blossom didn't recognise any of them as being local boys.

A few amused onlookers had gathered on the sea-wall overlooking the beach. They stood huddled together sharing one umbrella, amazed to see anyone attempting to swim in the rain. They would look even more amazed when they saw Blossom and Randolph climb the short ladder to get back into their house. For some reason people thought it extremely odd that anyone should actually have a home on the beach.

'Race you!' Blosssom started running. It wasn't far to go, the distance back to the ladder was about thirty yards. Although it was high tide the sea wasn't as far in today as it had been some weeks back. Then it had almost touched the wall at some points. They had been forced to remove the ladder lest it got swept away by the force of the waves. Randolph caught her up easily and overtook her, loping in long easy strides.

'Is there anything you can't do better than me?' she gasped on reaching the bottom of the ladder. 'It wouldn't have hurt to let me win that one, you cunt!'

He stood aside to let her up first and smacked her wet buttocks as they swayed past his hands.

'Ouch! That will show, it'll go all red!'

'I'll kiss it better.'

Blossom turned towards him. 'If you're not careful,' she said, 'you could be about to beat your own record.'

June reached Flowers just as Mercedes, the manageress of the hotel was leaving.

'Oh great – now I can have your cab –' Mercedes grinned, showing the attractive gap between her two front teeth. The taxi driver blinked at this stunningly exotic new fare, having only moments before given June up as a dead loss. He'd been wanting to show her off to his mates in the pub but she had claimed to have been in too much of a rush this evening. He

46

wondered if he might do a bit better with this black bird.

'You on the telly too, doll?' He hung out of his seat, eyeing the impressive length of Mercedes' legs. 'Look like a dancer to me –'

'Uh, uh – not any more, I'm not. Used to be years ago when I was a kid in Harlem.' Mercedes grinned at June again from behind her huge dark glasses. Their diamante-studded frames glittered against the deep brown of her skin. She was wearing her crinkly hair in many minute plaits, layered closely to the scalp and arranged in a set of circular ridges. It looked as though her head had actually been embroidered with a thickly encrusted pattern of black silk.

'I like your hair, Mercedes.'

'Gee thanks, honey – I only hope it does the trick. Cross fingers – I'm off for an audition. It's for the rape victim in something that's coming to the Royal Court. I think all the black actresses in Great Britain are up for it and the fucking part only calls for one pissy appearance!'

'Charming language!' The taxi driver was anxious to be off. The black bird was obviously out of his league, he could tell without trying. All those poncey actresses were the bleeding same.

June and Mercedes laughed.

'Good luck!' June waved and shouted.

Mercedes stuck her head out of the moving window. 'Masses of messages for you as usual – mostly all guys. Oh, yeah – your sister rang. I spoke to her, she seems kinda keen to have a chat with you sometime –'

That was one of the best things about living in a hotel, there was always someone to take the telephone calls. It seemed to June to be so much friendlier than simply having an impersonal answering service like all the other single people that she knew. And not only that, but it was altogether more cheerful a homecoming to be greeted by someone like Mercedes or one of the other girls on the desk. Rather than the cold silence of an empty flat.

Dimples was on the desk, she was Mercedes' second-in-command, a sweet-faced dumpling of a girl who everybody loved. Everybody, including a famous and married television comedian with whom Dimples had been having an affair for the last three years.

June greeted her now. 'Hello Dimples, I've just seen Mercedes looking fantastic – it only occurs to me – what an odd time to be holding auditions!' She glanced at the old, restored grandfather clock in the hall, beside the giant aspidistra plant. 'It's nearly seven o'clock.'

Dimples nodded and sighed. 'The audition is taking place in the writer's pad out in Islington.'

'Oh, it's one of those is it?'

'Sounds like it. Your sister's rung twice today. Loads of messages. Two party invites. Lucky thing, that's just what I could do with right now – a bloody good party. Thingy flew off to Las Vegas this morning, he won't be back for a month. At least he hasn't taken his missus with him – that I couldn't have bloody stood, the thought of the two of them out there together.'

June clucked sympathetically, taking the sheet of scribbled messages and quickly glancing over the list of written names. She had given up advising Dimples to put an end to the affair, but she still considered it an appalling waste, all the hanging around. It was perfectly obvious that 'Thingy' wasn't ever going to leave his wife and children for poor old Dimples. But she was helplessly in love that was the trouble, no one would have been able to persuade her to do without him. However unsatisfactory the arrangement.

'You could come to this party with me if you'd like to, that's if I decide to go. Loads of blokes there.' June pointed to one of the names.

Dimples eyes widened. 'Oh no – I'm only joking. He's ringing me anyway some time this evening so I'd have to be here. And I promised to hold the fort till Mercedes gets back, and goodness knows how long that's likely to be. But,' she laid her hand on June's and gave it a light squeeze, 'I do appreciate the thought – honestly.'

June gave up. It was useless trying to drag Dimples out, she'd tried before without success. 'Give me a ring in the room if you change your mind,' she said lightly, and turned to mount the stairs. 'Oh, if any calls come for me in the next half hour can you, tell them to ring back. I'm just going to have a bath now – but first I must have a word with Blossom. I've rung her twice today as well but the line's been engaged both times.'

'Perhaps it was her trying to get you. You have said that happens quite often with you two.' Dimples and Mercedes were as intrigued as everyone else with the idea of June having an identical twin, and were always longing for Blossom to come up to London so that they could actually see June's double for themselves.

'Either that or she and her sexy husband have been on the job all day – they always take the phone off the hook when they're at it.'

Dimples looked wistful. 'All day! Lucky for some – that's what I say.'

Blossom sounded positively radiant on the telephone. 'You just caught me in time – hold on. I'll go and turn the taps off, I've started running my bath . . . There's an opening tonight at the gallery – you know I told you that I'd done the big nude all in yellows and lemons to cheer up that empty wall above the bath –'

'The self-portrait, you mean?' June remembered. She was always surprised that Blossom didn't paint much more than she did. They had always been considered to have artistic talent. And it wasn't as if she hadn't all the time in the world at her disposal, with the children at school all day and Randolph locked away upstairs in his study. She never had been able to understand how on earth Blossom managed to while away the hours between getting up in the morning and going to bed. But then June had always been in a job. This afternoon Cherie had said that she was about to negotiate a contract for the Female series. If all went according to plan this major programme was scheduled to run for six weeks, later this spring, with June as the presenter. It would mark a definite advance in her career. And yet it struck her that she didn't have anyone close enough in her life with whom she could share this exciting news – except Blossom, of course. There would always be Blossom.

'That's the one, the self-portrait.' Blossom laughed infectiously. 'Well, nothing succeeds like success. Everybody loved it. So I did another one – all in bright greens to go above the red Aga in the kitchen. And Randy and Emily Shawl pursuaded me to send them both into the Society of Artists, though Pip and Willow made fun and said they would never get past the Hanging Committee. But they did! It's the first time that I've ever been hung!'

June congratulated her warmly, and then told her about the Female series.

'But that's *fabulous*, isn't it! Soon you'll become a household name — like, like Angela Rippon. No honestly you will, it's starting already. I can tell by the number of people who stare at me in the streets. Twice last week women stopped me to say that they had seen me on the telly — which reminds me. What about that Irish poet who was killed today — weren't you going over to interview him? We saw it on News at Six. A bomb explosion.'

'Actually it was his gas-stove.'

'No! Have they converted in Ireland yet?' Blossom sounded genuinely puzzled.

'What's Connor McConnors' exploding gas-stove to do with religion? You've lost me now, Blossom — ah, before I forget . . . I met an ardent admirer of yours at Chez Stalky's today. Professor Hamilton Hamilton.'

Blossom gasped. 'Oh, I think he is absolutely gorgeous, don't you! I meant converted to North Sea Gas. Yes, Hamilton came down here when Randy was writing *Understanding Understanding* — I was going to send you a copy. The translation is through now, but Randy said not to. It is a fearful bore. He said he wouldn't dream of inflicting it on his nearest and dearest.'

'Oh, but I'd like one, just to show off. Tell him I won't read it. Though, according to Professor Hamilton Hamilton, Randy is to get the Global Prize for it. Is that true? You didn't say.'

They spoke together for almost twenty minutes and would have gone on much longer but Blossom was mindful of the time.

'I'd best go,' she said excitedly. 'I'm cutting it a bit fine. We can't stay all that long at the opening, although it's my hour of glory. There's a darts match out at The Boozer's Gloom — poor old Randy's shitting himself already. He really needs to win tonight, it's getting near to the end of the darts season and he's lost as many as he's won. I think his own score is ten lost, ten won. They're all playing atrociously this year, the whole of The Boozer's Gloom team —'

'It's that old landlord, that old reprobate, that Gascoigne Teate. He casts the kibosh on everything.'

'Mm — terrific pub though — he makes it. And nobody would go if he wasn't there, and the darts night is the best of the week. It's the only night we drive out there now. Randy's working on something new. The rest of the week we just read or sit around watching television. I get the feeling sometimes that I'm really vegetating. What are you up to tonight? Out on a gay social round as usual? I shall be thinking of you dining somewhere very grand with Professor Hamilton Hamilton. Tomorrow night is our night for fish and chips – will you go to bed afterwards? I would if I were you. I must admit I was very tempted when he was down here.' Blossom gave an exaggerated sigh. 'But I worked it out that I had too much to lose – you haven't anything. It must be absolutely marvellous not to be weighed down with conscience, or hampered as I am by sexual loyalty.'

June was shocked. 'That's the first time I've heard you talk like that, Bloss!'

'I know – awful isn't it! It's the thought of you having it off with Professor Hamilton Hamilton – I was just remembering how horny his kisses made me feel . . .'

June lay in her hot bath sipping her cold drink. Glenfiddich on the rocks. It was interesting to note that no sooner had the icy alcohol hit her stomach but that she had the instant urge to empty her bladder. And that her urine as it trickled out seemed as chill as her drink. Yet it surely couldn't be whizzing straight through her system as swiftly as that, could it! She supposed that it was all to do with the temperature of the surrounding water. In the wintry sea, whenever she had accompanied Blossom and Randy on their daily swim, any personal water that she had passed had been a positive blessing of warmth and all too swiftly dispersing comfort. It had become a family joke. 'Quick, swim over here – the water's really warm!' June remembered now that she'd forgotten to ask Blossom if they'd been in today. Sometimes if Randy was working on something new, he preferred not to interrupt it with the swim and they would miss it for weeks on end. Blossom would never go in without him. She rarely did things on her own.

June studied her list of telephone calls and tried to decide what she would choose to do this evening. She had made a vague promise to Cherie Pye that she would look in at an informal gathering which Cherie was giving for another of her clients. A fashion journalist turned novelist who had become so successful that she was forced into being a tax-exile, and was choosing to flee to Dublin. June had met her once and they had, not disliked – but mistrusted each other on sight. Though she was sure that if they had the opportunity to get to know each other better they would probably end up as very good friends. It was not unusual for Cherie's clients to feel like this about each other. They were after all competing for Cherie's invaluable attention, like siblings clamouring for the mother.

But June did not feel drawn to the event. She had already lunched with her agent, leaving to share the Professor's taxi (needing just that little bit longer to effect a sure conquest). There was no way of guessing how Cherie's eating splurge had ended. She could be in an unpredictable mood by tonight. And it was possible to overdo things socially with Cherie, a little of her could go along way. She was very keen on raising the emotional temperature anyway, and the departure of the celebrated novelist would be larded with enough overtones of hysteria. June mentally crossed out the idea of going.

It was comfortable in the bath. That and the strong measure of Scotch were having an enervating effect upon her. She felt positively soporific now, wonderfully so. And it occurred to her that there was no earthly reason in the world why she should have to go out this evening at all. She would be missed – but not specifically. Not by any one person in particular. It was like that, her life. She was warmly welcomed wherever she went, but the sort of functions she attended didn't depend on her presence. Her circle of male friends were more like intimate strangers. In many cases she had only known them in bed.

Take the invitations for this evening for instance. One was for a private party, an impromptu affair, to follow the midnight screening of *The Wing of the Rat*. This was the latest science/fiction-cum-domestic/horror from the director of *The Snarl of the Dove*, and before that the hugely popular *The Smile of the Suckling Serpent*.

June had met the Czech director up in Scotland, whilst they were on location shooting *The Wing of the Rat*, but had been unable to cope with his sadism in the bedroom of the hotel where they both happened to be staying. He had abandoned her in highly embarrassing circumstances, so that the chambermaid had been forced to find extra help to free her. It had cost a fortune in tips. June hadn't found it in her heart to forgive him. And yet he continued to pursue her. She had inadvertently switched *Screen* on several nights ago (each of the hotel rooms were supplied with a colour television), and had just caught the start of an in-depth profile that was being done on him. The un-expected sight of the short, squat body and the square swarthy face had shocked in her a tremor of sexual excitement. She had forgotten how attractive she had found him. He had replied to the interviewer's questions in the same low, gentle, insidious voice that by the end of their night together she had learned to half dread. But on the television she thought it enormously seductive. Was it worth sexual humiliation however? June felt somewhere that it was like betraying the fight for female eman-cipation to allow oneself to be brutalised as a sexual object. She and Blossom always disagreed on that point.

The other party invitation (the one that she had suggested taking Dimples to) was being given in Valentine's Club, in Old Bond Street. Given by Valentine himself to celebrate the first birthday of the club. June had met Valentine in the Marbella Club in Spain when she had gone on a mad and mindless week-end with a girl called Amethyst, whose mother owned a villa out there.

Amethyst had been in love with Valentine, and when she had introduced him, June could understand why. He was im-mensely wealthy, and that appealed to a girl of Amethyst's social pretensions. He would inherit the title of his elder brother, should that brother die – which was more than likely. The brother had always been considered to be educationally sub-normal as a child, who now as a bachelor nearing his for-ties, had decided to take up motor-racing. His aim was to win the Grand Prix, he had already written off three racing vehicles and narrowly missed running over his own mechanic. But Valentine was altogether different.

When June had seen him first she had the immediate im-pression that he was a girl. A blonde, sun-tanned beauty with long curly hair drawn back and held with an elastic band at the nape of the neck. The smile had been as shy and as dreamy as a child barely awakened from sleep. Of course, he was stoned out of his mind at the time. And in no time at all so was she. All three of them had spent the night sleeping to-gether, curled in each other's arms on the hot beach. And in the morning Valentine had made love to each of the girls in turn. At the end of it June had fallen a little in love with him herself. But in spite of much pleading and many invitations from Amethyst on their return from Marbella, she had chosen not to repeat the experience. Then she and Amethyst had lost touch with each other, and June had completely forgotten the existence of Valentine. Until one night she had visited Valentine's Club after a party, with a whole crowd of people – not connecting her Valentine with this one – until he had seen her and asked her to dance. She had stayed with him for almost a fortnight before she (so he claimed) broke his heart by deciding to leave him.

By this time he had inherited the title. His brother had killed himself, and wiped out an entire family of peasants and two goats, whilst running in a new racer in Italy. June tried on the title for size. '*Lady* June – Lady *June* . . .' She took to mouthing it in the mirror, varying the emphasis on the different syllables. But try as she would she couldn't get it to sound like anything.

'I think it's the June – it's so *ordinary* there's no getting over it. Lady Blossom sounds *much* better. Just think, if I hadn't been dawdling about at the moment of our birth I could have ended up a bloody Lady.' Blossom had been appalled. 'You mean he's actually asked you to marry him, but you only re-met him last night – that was quick work, even for you! And you're thinking of turning him down, him *and* his title, because it doesn't sound right. Look, I'll come up and take your place, I'm not worried by how it sounds. And then at least we'll keep the title in the family.'

But it wasn't the Lady June part that had decided her in the end, she only wished she had more snobbery in her nature which would have made it easier to marry him purely for his title. The trouble really lay with the sort of life he would have expected them both to lead – it just smacked too much of the privileged and lazy lotus-eating. The richness of the diet was more than she could stomach.

It hadn't been altogether easy, leaving him. So feminine in appearance, even though his hair was now very short, he was an instinctive and sensitive lover. He made her feel more goddess-like than any of the others, touching her all the time and kissing those bare parts of her body that were visible to him when she was clothed. Her wrists. Her ears. Her eyelids. The nape of her neck. And her hair, he was always playing with her hair. Being perfectly content to lie beside her for hours twisting it around his long, thin fingers into tiny tendrils. Plaiting it, combing it, coaxing it into exaggerated styles, even washing it when she allowed him to (he was an inept hair-washer, dripping water all over the place).

'Are you a hair-fetishist, do you suppose, Valentine?' she had asked him seriously one day. They had spent all day in bed as they usually did, smoking joints (with June feeling as guilty as hell, being incommunicado from Cherie). Valentine had become so carried away by the sight of the perfect coiffure he had spent hours creating as she lay on her stomach reading a book that he had unexpectedly shot off between her shoulder blades.

'I adore and worship every inch of you,' came his trembling reply.

She had considered it rather an unsatisfactory answer to what was an interesting question.

But even the adoration had palled eventually, the pedestal proving to be a depressingly lonely place. And his sense of her increasing withdrawal only served to heighten the desperation of his passion. She had thought it best to make a clean break.

It was on nights like these, June reflected, that the disadvantages of being single seemed to be most apparent. Nothing would have been more pleasant at this very moment than to have someone else decide for her. Be there ready and waiting as she stepped out of her bath, with a soft fleecy towel to rub down her back. A quick answer to her query over what she should wear, and then the firm statement as to where they would be going. All decisions made with no prevarications. On the other hand . . . there was a late-night Joan Crawford film on the box; she was halfway through the new Patricia Highsmith; she had yet to try on the Italian, stiletto-heeled boots (bought this afternoon) with the rest of her wardrobe – nor had she had a chance to quietly plan out the line of her questions for tomorrow's confrontation with the eccentric Dame Tiger Oats . . .

June ran more hot water, and refilled her glass from the ice container and bottle of Glenfiddich that she had brought into the warm bathroom, for this very purpose. It was one of her very favourite occupations of all – getting gently and slowly completely smashed in the bath. She particularly liked what it inevitably led on to.

She took a strong steady draught of the fiery liquid between her lips and allowed it to rest, for as long as she could stand the burning sensation, upon her tongue. When she swallowed at last, it felt as though the entire inside of her mouth had been anaesthetized. She waited for the desired effect, it didn't take long. Whilst waiting, and still feeling relatively sober, she lathered and shaved both her legs, and carefully under each arm. She performed this slow ritual as if it were an erotic act, using a soft badger brush to produce the necessary profusion of thick, creamy bubbles from her solid, white square of scented soap. She could never remember the exact name of this soap, but had to save the wrapper; and each time she wanted to buy another she would produce the wrapper to show the assistant behind the counter. Always the same shop, a tiny *Parfumerie* off Shaftesbury Avenue, which displayed a prominent range of contraceptives. Once Valentine had accompanied her to the Shop (on one of their rare daylight jaunts), and had insisted on buying her perfume. The assistant, a frail, and friendly Hungarian in his late seventies, had insisted on calling his brother from the inner premises to decide which of their many perfumes would be the right one for the exquisite young lady. Valentine had been enchanted by the intricate ceremony of it all, and even June had felt flattered and beguiled. The perfume decided upon was *Bal à Versailles* worn, so it was claimed, by both the Queen of England (currently reigning) and Elizabeth Taylor. It was the most expensive perfume in the place. Immediately afterwards they had gone to the cinema, to the Curzon. Halfway through the film, one of Polanski's, June had thought that she was going to swoon. The extreme opulence and sinking comfort of the cinema seats, the decadence on the screen and the overwhelming and suffocating new scent had robbed her of all sense of reality. And Valentine was behaving so amorously. He was all over her – people were looking! He claimed the perfume had got under his skin. Since that time she had been very careful and sparing in its application. It was the only perfume she had ever worn that was infallible, it had never yet failed to arouse desire in men. This soap, its scent, had the same effect on her. Though it was quieter and less heady and somehow more private. And now the Scotch was doing its stuff too.

June sat up, her knees wide apart, and leaned between them towards the shower attachment on the shining chrome taps. She made the necessary adjustments to the temperature of the water and ferocity of its volume. And then, sinking languorously back into the luxuriant foam, she directed the strong spray from the shower straight to her clitoris.

This was one of the advantages of being single . . .

CHAPTER TWO

Blossom undulated along the deserted road that ran from the remote Maidens Cove over the moors to Puddlemouth. She was bare but for her bikini. Now and then a solitary vehicle would pass, slowing down to tempt the poor girl with a lift. The summer sun was already setting to the left, staining the sea and the sky with streaks of deepening red whilst retaining its own burning orange. The entire landscape was awash with this blooded reflection, even the blades of grass beneath Blossom's sandalled feet (thank Christ she had hung on to her sandals!). It was as if a celestial crime of violence had been committed, unleashing the floodgates of an unquenchable heavenly gore.

Blossom shivered but strode on, shoulders back in a brave though not convincing show of jauntiness. At the moment her flesh still held the heat of the day, but when the sun finally slunk beneath the line of the blurred horizon, she would quickly become chilled to the bone. She knew that. She knew also that very soon it would begin to get dark. And the darkness on these moors was quite unlike any other. Even those grown men of Cornwall who were noted for their courage, and who were completely familiar with the coves and cliffs around Puddlemouth, even they refused to venture over the moors after a certain hour of the night.

When Blossom and Randolph had first moved to these parts they had rented a small converted barn on the top of the cliffs. A remote and isolated spot which necessitated them owning two cars, one each. Then if one of them broke down or for some reason became delayed, the other person would not be completely abandoned. Blossom above all was deeply grateful for the arrangement, and felt that without it she would not have been able to survive. Her constant dread was that the time would come when, driving her small car over these moors, the engine would fail her, and she would be stranded, petrified in the unknown horrors of the night. Even in the daytime, in the safety of the speeding car, a sparkling blue beach-buggy with both babies strapped safely beside her, gurgling with happiness – even then she was uneasily aware of something unknown. Something dangerous and evil midst all that normality; something destructive. It was a deeply disquieting sensation of being menaced by the metaphysical.

She suddenly stumbled on a small stone, sliding to avoid the tangled roots of the bracken which grew in such malicious profusion. The bleak wind from the seas were so strong that the vegetation stood no chance of reaching any height. Everything grew close to the ground, crouched and crawling. Virulent – that was the word. Such trees as there were bore no leaves at all. They were thorny and black, hunched and bent all in the same direction with their backs to the cliffs. Like a sparse scattering of beckoning dwarfs. Grotesque and frightening.

Blossom was frightened now, conscious that in this situation her vivid imagination was going to be her worst enemy. She should have accepted the lifts that had been offered instead of this ludicrous show of independence. Now she regretted her own stupidity and the suspicions that had prompted her refusals. Surely the possible rape by a fellow human would be preferable to this savagery of the senses . . .

She resolved to take the very next car that came along. But where was it? One would come in a minute. She had no watch, but she knew perfectly well that the coves and beaches would be empty by now. When she had scrambled away from Maidens Cove there were very few people left.

But one car must come soon, she was confident of that – wasn't she? In the meantime she must stride along, showing a brave face, her best foot forward And above all, concentrate her thoughts on matters of absolute normality. After all whose bloody fault was it that she was in this bizarre situation – she had only herself to blame.

The car, when it came, was long and low, a malevolent black. It crept behind her so noiselessly that she hadn't known it was there until it had passed her and purred to a halt a few yards ahead. But at that point she harboured no misgivings, she was so thankful that it had appeared at all.

She ran forward, her breasts jiggling; the cold had got to them now and both nipples were erect. There was nothing she

5

could do about them except cross her arms over her chest like a self-conscious schoolgirl. Perhaps this man at the wheel would have a car rug with which she could cover herself. It looked the kind of car that would have that sort of luxury.

Ahead of her the door of the heavy vehicle swung silently open. She caught the glimpse of a powerful male wrist upon which was strapped a skin-diver's watch.

She drew level and bent down, a smile of gratitude on her lips.

The malignant moors bore sullen witness to the savage seduction.

'In my opinion you took far too long – I was shivering by the time you drove up! And it was nearly dark, there were bats about – I was getting really scared, you sod!' Blossom beamed delightedly across at her husband.

She lay, reclining across her latest acquisition – a magnificent tiger-skin rug, complete with head. She was attired in a black satin nightdress, side-slit to the waist. Its bodice was composed of inky intricate lace through which her breasts gleamed like luminous eggs. The matching negligé, edged with a froth of maribou feathers, fell nonchalantly about her shoulders, providing a striking frame for the curve of her uncluttered neck, free now of the hair so recently shorn. The new hair colour, a soot black, suited her eyes. It gave her, more than ever, the appearance of a sleek feline, but now with a touch of the witch. A femme fatale, that's what it felt like. The chic cropped dense hair – as if she was wearing a raven's wing, a symbol of black magic above her brow. No other hair colour had made her react to herself quite so strongly. And June had admitted to having the same feelings! Not so strange really – though this time Blossom had hoped for once to surprise her twin.

'I've had my hair done, it's completely different . . .'

'So is mine. I was going to keep it a secret till you next saw me – you'll have quite a shock . . .'

'So will you. Mine's black . . .'

'No! So's mine! Black and very short . . .'

'Short – so is mine . . .'

They had both laughed. There could be no surprise – that was the way it always was.

Randolph was reading, deliberately withholding attention

from his wife – the attention which she so eagerly sought. She pouted and put on a little girl voice, pouring herself a fresh glass of champagne and popping another soft-centre in her mouth (Best go easy on these – she'd already exceeded her daily calorie count. But this role demanded a fair amount of self-indulgence. She was playing the part of a tired businessman's plaything).

'You're not listening to your baby.' She wriggled seductively, cupping her breasts, one in each hand, as if offering them on a plate. Randolph sighed heavily and lay down his *Financial Times*. It was a paper that he never normally would have dreamed of glancing at. Blossom had bought it this morning for a touch of authenticity.

He frowned at her, drawing on his thick cigar. (The role was to his liking in this respect – it enabled him to have a bloody good smoke. A rare enough event. He and Blossom had given up eighteen months before.)

'I hardly regard this to be in order.' It had been agreed that this mogul should display a broad streak of pomposity.

'What's that, pet?' Blossom widened her eyes innocently à la Marilyn Monroe. She continued to hold onto her firm jutting breasts, now squeezing them lightly and pressing them to her with the palms of her hands. As she did so, her cleavage deepened in the delicate lace. The swelling overspill threatened to break the cobwebby boundaries. She could see that her mammary mime was having the desired effect by the tautening bulge in his trousers.

'Gradual Expansion? Or,' she pointed, 'Increasing Inflation?' This was the businessman's jargon.

Randolph crossed his legs with a certain discomfort. 'I hardly regard this to be in order.' Along with the pomposity was a tedious tendency towards repetition. He continued unperturbed, as if he were unaffected by the sight of Blossom brazenly scooping both nipples out and trying to squash them towards each other so that they met.

'Look darling – rubbing noses!' She dimpled ingenuously. 'Would you care to? It doesn't hurt, honestly!'

Randolph coughed and cleared his throat of the rushing saliva. 'I hardly regard this to be in order,' he began importantly. 'This reference to the events of the afternoon. It is a question of etiquette. One has no wish to be acquainted with your activitites outside this bedroom. Might I suggest that it is more than a trifle indelicate, if not to say painful for me to have to imagine you in the arms of another man.'

Blossom jabbed at an almond cream, it was not her favourite flavour. She was more fortunate with her next choice. Coffee. She grinned happily. 'It was a *hell* of a poke – it took four and a half minutes from entry to orgasm. I timed it on your watch. Woosh, straight in! A completely dry run, no foreplay – I've rather taken to rape lately. Have you noticed we . . .'

Randolph laid his cigar down with an air of resigned exasperation. 'I'm giving up,' he said testily. 'You're not concentrating tonight. Since when have we agreed to start mixing our sexual metaphors? You can't be in two roles at once, this isn't a rehearsal. If you need an interval or a half time you have to announce it . . .'

'Sorry, sorry, sorry, my darling – I must be getting excited, that's what it is!' Blossom writhed seductively over to where he sat and insinuated her arms between his crossed legs, until she had gently prised them apart. Now his erection was such that it formed a third limb, though marginally shorter – and lacking a foot and five toes.

'How do you do,' she said, shaking its head.

Randolph gave a low groan.

She bent her head down towards the pale pink chequered trousers. Cool for summer and drip-dry. Manufactured in the States but actually sold over here in Harrods. 'I love these pants,' she murmured softly. And she began slowly kissing the tip of the visibly outlined glans. Randolph shuddered, unable to control the tiny tear of spunk that he guessed to be leaking from his extremity. The start of the action – for purposes of lubrication.

But it was lost – a mere spit in the ocean of Blossom's saliva. To his alarm it was becoming obvious that his wife's sexual inventiveness was now leading her to actually suck him off *through his togs*!

It must be the material, the brand name of the fabric, that had sown the seed of the idea in her mind. Seersucker. They had made a private joke of it after the Harrods' assistant had praised the practical advantages of Seersucker as summerwear. But, Jesus, it hadn't crossed Randolph's mind that it might come to this!

He re-lit his cigar and, despite himself, *squirmed*. Blossom, her mouth full of drip-dry, had now engineered her body into such a rum position that she was managing to maintain a permanent contact between her clitoris and his knee-cap. He had best not bend his leg, lest he lose his whole shin and shank. He still remembered the time that Blossom had made vigorous use of his left elbow as a masturbatory aid, and the irrational terror that, starting with that simple joint, his entire body might be sucked into hers. The primitive fear of castration of course – and yet he had never experienced this during fellatio. Even now, climbing closer and closer to climax, with Blossom's strong jaw clamped to his crotch, her teeth worrying his cock like a terrier with a bone, or a bird with a worm, it was still that trapped knee that caused him uneasiness. Even through the puckered material of the Seersucker and despite the fact that the surface of the knee is not ordinarily sensitive to degrees of temperature (tough elbows by contrast, are the testing instruments for the bath-water of a baby), Randolph was nervously aware of the moist warmth of what felt like Blossom's yawning chasm. He could only pray that he wouldn't fall in. Meanwhile Blossom was enjoying herself enormously.

It was true that she was excited. She had been excited all month, ever since it had been arranged that she should take a holiday with June. Tomorrow she would be in London! It was two years since she had last been up, and then only on an overnight stay. Willow had developed the sure symptoms of measles within minutes of Blossom's train leaving the station. It was obvious to everyone that Randolph was incapable of coping with the situation, even though it had been arranged that Emily Shawl's Pots would be taking care of the children in Blossom's absence. This summer they, Pip and Willow, were camping with their friends and family in the Dordogne. They had begged to be allowed to go, even though it meant that they would be away from home for practically their entire school holiday.

'Six weeks! That's how long it means – doesn't it concern you at all that our own flesh and blood can exist quite happily for that long without seeing us?' Blossom had agonised privately to Randolph.

'Certainly not!' he had answered without hesitation. 'It'll be marvellous to see the back of the little sods . . .'

'Randy!' She had reproached him. Why? She couldn't have explained . But she felt that surely, as parents, it was their duty to at least examine how they stood with their children from time to time. Wasn't this about the age when the generation gap would soon start making itself felt? Shouldn't they be preparing themselves for the eventuality of strife and trouble. Or was it foolish to anticipate trouble in this way – thus turning it into a reality. Randolph thought so.

'We'll meet it head-on when it happens, old girl –'

'Don't old girl me.'

'Why not? You're behaving like an old girl. Fusspotting. For want of something to occupy your mind.'

'You patronising turd!'

'It's perfecly true and you know it. Your children are growing up, you feel threatened by their increasing signs of independence. It causes you to question your own identity and consider . . .'

'I know what it causes me . . .'

'Ah, now we're getting somewhere.'

'It causes me to want to hit you hard across the mouth, you pontificating bore . . .'

But her holiday with June had been Randolph's idea. He was not a believer in holidays himself, he didn't see the point of them. 'Tell me,' he would declaim, sweeping his arms about to encompass the raging ocean to his right, and the magnificence of his library on his left. 'Tell me where on holiday I would find these?'

Blossom never bothered to reply, in a way she agreed with him. It was only lately that the idea of a *change* had begun to appeal to her. Perhaps this was what Randolph had been quick to sense though she had certainly not put it into words.

'You should go away and spend some time with June.' That was what he had said. 'The change will do you good.' It would be their first real parting for years and years. The last time had been when he had been invited to address a literary Symposium in Stuttgart. It had been arranged then that Blossom would accompany him, but at the very last moment it had proved impossible. Pip had fallen and broken the bridge of his nose, and though there was no fear of permanent damage or complication at the time, the small boy was nevertheless very shaken. As was Blossom. She couldn't find it in her heart to leave him. It was a bitter disappointment, but it couldn't be helped.

Randolph had taken the opportunity of having a brief and

unsatisfactory four-day affair with a woman, whose name he read regularly of late as a contributor to the TLS. Each time it never failed to bring a small jolt of guilt. He had returned more in love with Blossom than ever, and fiercely protective concerning this love. Above all he was determined that she should be spared the painful knowledge of his betrayals. For there had been others at various times, though each had occurred when he was away from home, when he had been at his most vulnerable simply though missing Blossom. And all that each experience had served to do was make him more than ever aware of her worth. But, though he didn't reasonably doubt her forgiveness for a moment, a further wisdom forewarned that the intimacy between them would ultimately suffer if she found out. His marriage was too precious and important to allow that to happen. This made him doubly careful over his indiscretions. In short – he didn't play the irresponsible bloody fool. He was as devious as the next randy bastard.

Or would be – if Blossom allowed there to be anything salvaged from her assiduous syphoning system. Without admitting it to himself he would quite relish the rest when she went up to London to join June tomorrow. It would give him a real chance to devote himself to uninterrupted thought. It could not be denied that Blossom was an ever-present and disturbing distraction. And delightful though that was, he quite looked forward to leading the temporary life of a monk. He must look up under A-abuse, bodily; in his Ecclesiastical section as to which Order took a lenient line on wanking.

Blossom wriggled provocatively. To Randolph's relief, she had abandoned his knee-cap (beneath the drenched trouser-leg) as a means of sexual stimulation. But – now he feared for his lit cigar – she seemed occupied in fresh and possibly more alarming endeavours. He couldn't be sure but she seemed to be stuffing herself, as he had seen her stuff chickens or turkeys for Christmas – what the devil . . .!!

She gave him no time for further conjecture. Before he'd had a chance to restore order to his whirling thoughts, she had completely reversed the direction of her whole body. One minute facing south she was suddenly facing north! How she had managed to do this without once releasing his saliva-saturated crotch and its burgeoning contents from her teeth was a positive miracle. He found time to offer up a small prayer that the whole caboodle hadn't been bitten clean away! And now that fear, primitive and fierce, was proving a galvanising force . . . the ejaculation was here . . . the searing, soaring, spinning had begun . . .

He opened his mouth wide in an animal groan of rapturous pain.

Blossom sank her haunches to his rigid tongue. He came, gagging horribly on a sickly combination of hazelnut-fudge and chocolate crystallized ginger.

Blossom was leaving in the morning on the five o'clock train. 'Christ Almighty, five o'clock in the fucking morning! What sort of train is that!' Randolph drove everywhere in his powerful motor on his rare trips away. It was ages since he'd been on a train. But between them, Blossom and June had decided that she should come by train instead of prevailing on Randolph to drive her up. Or indeed driving that long way herself (on moving into Puddlemouth from their previous isolated habitation on the moors, Blossom had got rid of her beach-buggy. Though not without a twinge or regret for the loss of independence that this meant. She resented having to *ask* for anything of his – however sweetly he responded). As yet the girls had not decided how they were going to spend their time together, or what sort of holiday they would like to have. But if it called for a car, hiring one would be no problem. Both were experienced drivers, with their licences all in order. The only reason that June didn't run a car of her own was that London had become so impossible for parking, and anyway it was just as easy to take taxis.

'What sort of train? The sort that gets me into London as early in the morning as possible. Ten o'clock, that's when it gets to Paddington.'

Blossom had consulted her timetable. 'Actually, no. Ten forty-two, it says here I must give June a ring, I think I've given her the wrong time. She's meeting me, I'll need a hand with all my baggage.'

Randolph had begun to regard the trip with a certain apprehension. He didn't look forward to heaving six very heavy cases at the god-forsaken hour of five in the morning. Although it was perfectly true that he rose earlier than most, he did so because he considered those to be the most valuable contemplative stages of the day. The dawn. That precious and too fleeting metamorphosis of darkness to light, of blindness to sight, of a world cloaked and concealed beneath a blanket of blackness trembling in paler and paler transition to the radiance of the full spectrum of light. It filled him with awe, this birth of the day. It inspired him and lent a sense of pure magic to the following hours.

And now he was to be called upon to hop into the car, check the choke, charge the engine, drive his departing wife to the station, humping her grotesquely heavy suitcases onto the train (endangering his dodgy back in the process) and stand like a dolt waving on the platform till her sweet suntanned face was but a dot in the distance. All the time the dawn would be breaking. Without him.

'I don't expect you to drive me to the station, my darling.'

Good God – could she read every thought in his head!

'I've already arranged with Wally Cronk to pick me up at about four-thirty. He's the best one for the cases. . . .'

'What old Nelson, with his one arm?' Randolph was trying hard not to reveal his intense relief.

'Two. He's got two now. He's had a marvellous contraption fitted. Like a miniature crane – with a lever, for lifting things. And a steel hand at the end of it, it's the very latest thing. Much better than a human hand in his line of business – he was telling me he's made a fortune this summer, with part-time porterage and the car-hire. So you can commune with the dawn undisturbed, and I'd prefer not to have you seeing me off actually. It would make it all too emotional.'

Randolph was moved. God, he loved her!

Blossom lay awake unable to sleep, her mounting excitement meant that every half hour she was having to get up to check her luggage to see that she had packed various things which kept occurring to her over-active brain. At times she felt as though she would explode with the tension. Keep calm, cool it, kid – she kept saying to herself. But it was no use, rational thinking was out of the question. In the end she just lay there awaiting the alarm, cuddling her unconscious husband.

From time to time she kissed him lightly, all over his face, lingering at the relaxed and slightly open lips, but he didn't stir. Nothing would have woken him, not even the alarm. When it went off, at four o'clock, his regular breathing remained unchanged. His sleeping hours ran strictly to habit. Knowing this they had made their passionate and fond farewells before going to bed. Blossom would depart like a thief in the night. Randolph would awake at his usual time to find her gone.

June waited at the barrier on Paddington Station feeling like death. She only wished that people would stop staring at her. Although she was wearing a large pair of dark glasses and a deep-brimmed black hat, beneath which she would have thought it was possible to hide, passers-by apparently still recognised her. Of course they were glancing in the first place, she knew perfectly well, because she looked so bloody stylish. These days she was dressing completely in black and white, from top to toe, not a smattering of colour anywhere. Except on her lips and nails (finger and toe) which were painted a deep shade of coffee, bordering on crimson. They had worked it out together, she and Cyril, the wonderful old pouf who was the designer on her television series.

Her new look, which though admired greatly by Cherie Pye, Mercedes and the girls in Make Up, had been greeted with some reserve by the male director of the series, and by almost all the camera crew. They thought it too strange, even slightly alienating for the public. In their opinion a presenter should be someone with whom the viewers should be able to identify, not someone who looked like Dracula's mother!

But Publicity had disagreed. The three typists and two secretaries had already adopted the look, and adapted it to themselves. June had cropped her hair very short, leaving a very long fringe which sometimes she swept severely to the side like a boy's. And at other times she combed it straight down her forehead almost into her eyes. Or else frivolously curled it into a bubble of curls, like a '50's musical comedy star. Each style suited her rather long, pointed face, pinpointing the drama of the smouldering eyes. And the colour emphasised the neat outline of the head and the chic-ness of the style. And of course she was also very tanned.

June's method of tanning was one she had devised several years before when she had returned from a continental holiday, disappointingly pale. The Italian sun had put in only two appearances throughout her ten-day stay. Rather than risk being the laughing stock of the office, or the object of pity for all her friends — not to mention the permanently sun-tanned Blossom — she thought of a clever deception. Returning half a day sooner than she was expected, she booked a two-hour appointment at the Beauty Salon in South Kensington. There she received their Instant Tan Treatment, consisting of a thorough over-all creaming of tanning lotion applied by a qualified masseuse. She emerged, slightly sweaty (a side effect of the lotion) but with a deep and thoroughly convincing mediterranean suntan. Then after a leisurely lunch in an out of the way restaurant, where she had a bothersome time with both Cypriot waiters who assumed she was one of their own race, she had returned to the place where she was staying (this was during one of her 'off' times with Tiny), and rang everyone to say, 'Hello — I'm home!'

She had employed the same ruse each summer since then, and this year had even hit on the idea of having herself tanned in the winter — just after Christmas, when her spirits were in need of a quick lift. It was most gratifying to be congratulated in January on her suntan. Everybody just assumed that she had been skiing at some smart winter resort. Even the more casual of her lovers thought this — those that she went several weeks without seeing. She'd been sunning, because she had simply been creamed in the face, neck and hands — the only parts that are bared in the snow. Similarly in the summer she had donned her bikini, so that those bits of her body had remained white.

This year she had decided to adopt a topless tan. She had forgotten to tell Blossom how aroused she had been as the very attractive cockney masseuse had smoothed the slippery cream over her breasts. 'Do you fancy your nipples?' The girl had asked her ingenuously. June would have loved to have asked her, 'Do you?' but she feared that it might be misconstrued and, she didn't want to become known as having lesbian tendencies, not when she visited the Salon so regularly. She had overheard snatches of derogatory gossip about other clients who on the surface appeared the models of propriety and absolute sexual normality. The cutting comments had seemed to her to be unnecessarily censorious and cruel. But this was South Kensington after all. You would have to travel a few miles further in each direction to find the more raffish element in which she found herself more at ease. 'How do you mean – my nipples?' The girl was tweaking them already, holding the entire breast between both hands and employing a firm whirling motion. It was as much as June could do to simply shut her eyes and lie on the sweetly clean-towelled surface of the couch – smiling. Smiling a sensual smile of absorption. She was beginning to feel unforgiveably horny. 'Well, I only ask,' the girl spoke without any trace of self-consciousness. If anything she sounded just a trace too officious for June's liking. 'I only ask because some of our clients prefer not to be touched up here.' She touched June's stiffened nipples with a delicate flip. 'But I can tell that it doesn't worry you at all. Funny thing, that. But then you have all sorts come in here – I couldn't begin to tell you half of it, honestly! Are you married? No, of course you're not. Well, some of the married ladies are amongst the worst, believe you me.' June nodded, trying to control the drowsy and wholly delightful feeling that she was experiencing as a direct result of the girl's finger-tips on her nipples (did nipples go that much browner anyway in the sun? She must remember to check with Blossom, who this year had taken to this topless lark too.) 'You'd think, wouldn't you that they'd be satisfied with their husbands?' The girl paused, pondering on her own considered opinion. Her mind no longer wholly on what she was doing, she had bunched her finger-tips over each of June's nipples and was idly caressing them, using the tentative touch of a safe-breaker. It was becoming unbearable. June could feel her expression slipping into one of hollow-eyed lewdness, with a permanent lopsided grin pasted in place. Despite herself she found that she was crossing her legs. But not for long. The girl snapped back into action. 'Miss Day! Whatever do you think you're doing – the lotion hasn't had time to take on those legs yet! Now I shall have to give them another coat otherwise they'll smear. What on earth could you have been thinking of to do such a thing?' June chose to apologise, rather than confess.

Blossom's train was going to be twenty minutes late due to an unforeseeable delay on the line. June groaned as it was announced, as did others in the small group waiting beside her. One of them, a middle-aged woman with an unflattering henna rinse on her grey hair, turned to June and raised her hands despairingly. But June looked away, refusing to be drawn into any sort of exchange with the woman who had been covertly eyeing her from a distance for the last five minutes or so.

The trouble was that last night the second of the series had been transmitted, which was why June was being recognised this morning. Her face was still fresh on people's minds. Last week, with the first, it had been exactly the same the following day. But even by the weekend the interest had fallen away.

Contrary to how she thought she'd feel she didn't altogether enjoy the continual goggling. There were times, like this morning when feeling as she did, she would have infinitely preferred to be able to move around the world anonymously. She didn't relish the thought of five further weeks of this and worse to come when the series became nationally networked. Then her soul wouldn't be called her own. Already there were small indications that this was about to happen. Yesterday the *Guardian* had rung for an exclusive interview with her. Publicity had been forced to reply that for the moment June Day was giving no interviews at all. It was a pre-arranged policy, a group decision by all participants in the Female Series that they should work as a collective. No one was to receive more acclaim for their part in the proceedings than anyone else – the presenter included. The success of the series was almost wholly due to this magnificent group spirit. And this was to be so until the present screening had been concluded.

But other signs were starting to appear. June's name had appeared twice in the same week in the gossip column of the *Evening Standard's* Londoners' Diary. Each time her name was linked with different male escorts, Professor Hamilton being one of them. He had been extremely displeased over the others.

Also the beauty editor of *Vogue* had been trying to persuade Publicity that the inclusion of June's photograph in an article on contemporary faces would not violate the no-interview embargo. Similarly with the fashion editor of one of the Sunday colour supplements who wished to do a coverage of June's black and white wardrobe. It all looked like the start of a positive avalanche of personal publicity. June was at a loss to explain her lack of enthusiasm. She could only think that she must be in need, in desperate need of a holiday. That was why she had so welcomed the suggestion from Blossom. She wondered about that. It was the first time that Blossom and Randolph would have willingly been apart – not that their marriage was in any faintest way less than secure . . . She wouldn't have minded

71

having a marriage that happy – who would indeed? She thought of her colleagues in Television Towers, not one decent marriage between them. It must be the hours, or the pressure, the constant living on the edge of the nerves. That's what did it. The ceaseless flow of adrenalin. Only last week nice Nobs Plater had complained of chest pains. Rather appalling ones, so he claimed. 'Perhaps you just experienced your first coronary, Plater old chap!' a fellow newscaster had cried with an over-jovial thump between the shoulder blades. The hearty blow had sent the shaky Nobs reeling in the direction of the nearest seat. Onlookers had been secretly appalled by the callousness of the sentiment.

Twenty minutes delay – well, it gave June the chance to buy all the papers and glance through them over a cup of ghastly coffee in the station buffet. She had risen at the last possible moment this morning. She must be sickening for something to feel this weak, this queasy. Perhaps it was the summer flu bug that had been flying round the studio floor. It wouldn't make much of a welcome for Blossom, but she honestly felt that she should go back to bed. She was feeling worse by the minute.

She had meant to ring Cherie this morning. They had arranged between them that June would call before eleven. But she hadn't done so. She hadn't felt up to Cherie's particular brand of continental vivacity, not in her present state of health. It wasn't even as if she had been out on the toot last night either. It had been lights out by eleven, she had felt unutterably weary. It had obviously been this bug thing coming on.

Ten more minutes left. June glanced at her watch. There had been an encouraging review of the programme in *The Times*, with a special congratulation for herself. And a typical throw-away line in the *Sun* describing her as 'a tasty TV dish – the sort that any man would like to have on his knees!' There was nothing in the rest of the newspapers so June barely bothered with them. There you are, she caught herself up with a small jolt, you dismiss them as being of no particular interest. Simply because you, or your programme are not in them. Better begin to control the old ego!

But her eyes ached unbearably, and the effort of reading had thoroughly exhausted her. Nine more minutes. She thought of Cherie and how irritated she would be if June didn't ring. There would most certainly be a call put through to Flowers which would be awaiting her return. She may as well get it over with now.

The secretary answered as soon as the switchboard had put her through. 'Hello June – I'm sorry but Cherie hasn't arrived yet, I've been expecting her for the past hour.' Cherie ran a very democratic office, everyone was on christian-name terms. 'But as you probably know,' the secretary lowered her voice, 'she was seeing Samson last night. I should think that must have something to do with her non-appearance, wouldn't you . . .' The tone of her conversation suddenly altered, 'Good morning, Cherie! I have June on the line. She's ringing from Paddington, you remember that she is meeting her twin there this morning. I trust,' June could almost hear the twinkle in the voice, 'I trust that you had a good evening with . . .'

'With that 'orrible 'usband of mine! 'Ow I 'ate 'im! *Mon Dieu*! This time I shall most definitely 'ave to 'ave a divorce – there is no other way. You would please to get my lawyer on the phone for an appointment – this farce has gone quite far enough!'

June held the receiver away from her head, the seconds were slipping away but Cherie's shrill excitable delivery was slicing across her quivering nerve-ends. Her scalp started throbbing with sharp needles of pain, but just in one spot above her left temple. She would have to take a couple of Panadol, much as she loathed tablets, or pills of any kind.

Six more minutes before the train was due to arrive. The pips in the pay-phone would start at any second and June had forgotten to check that she had enough change to continue talking. Cherie must have had a sixth sense. 'Ma petite – you are in a 'orrible coin-box. You give me the number quick and I shall be ringing you back by return. Otherwise those peep-peep-peeps 'ave to cut us off.'

June gave the number, she felt too weak to refuse. Even bursting with health and absolutely in the pink it would have been difficult to refuse Cherie. And from where she stood she had a clear view of the platform. When Cherie's call came through there were four minutes left.

Four minutes more. Blossom checked her watch. Was there time to pay yet another (surely her fifth) visit to the lavatory? It amazed her that there would be anything left, of any substance, to evacuate from her exhausted bowels. It had become positively embarrassing towards the end of the journey, her constant trek past the same fellow passengers. So much so that she had been forced to alternate the direction of her visits, swaying first to the fore of the train, and then to the rear. Even once, when she imagined there to be raised eyebrows and meaningful glances between a married pair sitting closest to the TOILET – VACANT/ENGAGED sign, she had pretended to be on her way to the buffet car. She had returned after a particularly belly-curdling bout with an undrinkable waxy carton of British Rail tea in her hand. She had a horror of being thought incontinent. There wasn't time. Blossom clenched her teeth and forced herself to gaze on the fleeting suburban landscape whizzing past the window. She had never shared everyone else's scathing view of suburbia. To her there was something solid and deeply comforting in the sight of row upon row of identical homes, backed as they were with their precious little gardens. It fascinated her, the differences between these small plots. It proved how creative an animal man was to shape squares and oblongs of immaculate grass until they were as smooth and as evenly green as the surface of a billiard table; to trim hedges, train creepers, to tidy up trees; to impose his intelligence upon the disorderliness of nature; to cultivate vegetables and take care of raw and unripened fruits until they reached rich succulence; and the blooms, the fabulous flowers. Now, at the height of summer Blossom was seeing the flowers at their best. The marigold, the lily, the lilac, the pink; the antirrhinum, the gladiolus, and the spectacular and wholly ravishing rose – all those pistils and stamens, and corolla and calyx! Blossom marvelled at the hours of industry and dedication.

Of course she didn't have a garden, they had never had one, she and Randolph. They preferred the beach and ocean as a back yard. And in the end those took infinitely less of one's time – a garden after all was very time-consuming.

Two minutes to go! Blossom doubled up over a violent spasm of pain in her gut. Good God – she was behaving like an overexcited child. If Pip or Willow had displayed these symptoms she would have been seriously concerned that she had bred a neurotic. But they hadn't a twin. They couldn't possibly know what immeasurable pleasure – no, something much, much stronger and deeper than that, was consuming her now. Now when the minute was here, the actual moment, the split second . . .

Blossom put her head out of the window as the train shuddered to a grinding halt. She opened the door and stepped onto the platform. A flying form rushed towards her. She had time only to glimpse the face, *her* face, her own. *Her* body, *her* hands. It was as if she were embracing *her* self.

'So tell me what's with you and Professor Hamilton Hamilton – I haven't had all the latest on that yet.' Blossom perched on the curve of June's circular bed, preferring it to the canvas director's chair which was the only other seat in the room, apart from the bean-bag, a tough crimson sack intended to mould to the body when sat in. Blossom had two of them at home, now relegated to the children's rooms, as being entirely unsuitable for adult frames. Randolph had thrown his spine out completely one Wednesday night, watching Panorama with a Pimms in one hand and Roget's *Thesaurus* in the other as light reading (during the yawning parts of Panorama). To Blossom's alarm he had been unable to move a muscle at the end except his face and neck which were contorting horribly. It was as if he had become *at one* with the bean bag. Had he been able to stand, the bean-bag looked as though it would rise with him like some obscene livid growth. Doomed to live out his days as a card-carrying hunchback! The tragic yet trite image flashing before her eyes had made Blossom chuckle. Unfortunately Randolph, in his agony, had chosen that precise moment to glance up. It was months before he could find it in himself to forgive what he viewed as her crass derision at the sight of a loved one's distress.

June was in the bed propped up with pillows, a glass of hot honey and whisky held in her mittened hands, her throat muffled in the fluffy comfort of an Angora scarf. She was wearing a voluminous flannelette long sleeved nightgown, once the property of Emily Shawl's deceased maiden aunt. Blossom was playing Mother. She wasn't drinking, she didn't want to get drunk this early in the day. As soon as she had got June nicely settled and tucked up she had planned to sail out on a little shopping spree. She was very taken with June's black and white wardrobe and had thought of doubling up on several of the items for herself.

6

But first she couldn't resist the opportunity for a gossip. In no time at all June would be asleep – the best thing for this sort of bug. With luck she might be up and about tomorrow, but the rest of today was out of the question. Blossom had swallowed her disappointment. All the way up in the train she had been fantasizing over where they would be lunching, which film they'd see, with whom they'd have dinner, which night-club they might end up dancing in . . . She'd been racking her brains, trying to recall where it was that Bianca Jagger was always dancing cheek-to-cheek with different people. And she had touched her own cheek to test its possible pressability (against that of an, as yet un-met, male cheek).

Now she had come to terms with it. In any case her burgeoning maternal instinct had dictated the rest. Her sister, poor love, was decidedly under the weather. Anyway there was plenty of time for all the high-jinks, after all she would be away from home for a fortnight!

June moved her eyes although it pained her to do so, the sockets felt as though they had been filled with wet cement and left to harden. She waved a weak mitten towards the minute balcony beyond the french window, through which the full blast of summer sun shone. The balcony overhung a typical London scene – the conventional communal garden. This was already languidly alive with parked prams and young mothers strolling and smiling indulgently at small toddlers in sandpits. Thank Christ, that's all over – Blossom found herself thinking – all over for me. Finished. In the past. She knew that she would never have another child.

'What is it, angel? Do you want the blinds down? I'll do it, the light's too strong for your eyes. You'd best get off to sleep. That's it – snuggle down. We've got masses of time for a good gossip. Oh, are you sure you don't mind if I wear your white dress, and borrow that little black peaked hat? I shall probably buy the patent sandals first, before going for the clothes, and I'll get a better idea of how they look together. I've got the list of places. Now you take care of yourself. If you like I'll come back around lunchtime, to see how you are . . .'

June shook her head vigorously, an action she immediately regretted. She ached in every single strand of her short hair. Unbidden tears sprang to her eyes. Blossom was so sweet and solicitous, it suddenly made her see what she had been missing

– someone to fuss over her at times like these. Someone who *cared* even when she looked (as she knew she did now) positively hideous, a disgrace to the human race. She flapped a feeble mitten gesturing Blossom to her, catching her sister's hand and pressing it with her honey-sticky lips. Blossom kept a judicial distance (it wouldn't do at all to catch this bloody bug – she had no wish to spend her precious holiday in bed).

'Now my chicken, don't upset yourself, just keep nice and warm. The thing is to sweat it out. I know with the kids.'

When Blossom left, June buried her face into the pillow, sobbing. It was as if someone had turned off the light, or brutally sliced her in two.

It started happening right away, as soon as Blossom got into the lift. An American girl with a tangle of bleached curls and a bare sunburnt midriff, whose neck was festooned with highly professional looking camera equipment, hailed her. 'Hi there, Junie – we caught your show last night! You were really something! I tell you when you caught that guy bawling out that broad – whew, I thought "sister have you got him nailed"! Yup, just by the fuckin' balls!' She screwed up her short bobbed nose (a nice job, whoever had done it) and twisted her clenched fists as though she was wringing water out of a wet towel. Blossom winced inwardly and felt instant sympathy for the owner of the threatened genitals.

The American girl didn't stop talking until the lift hit the ground floor, so that although Blossom had opened her mouth to explain that it was a case of mistaken identity and that she was not Junie at all, but her identical twin, she was simply not given the chance. 'Well, 'bye Junie – see ya . . .' The girl flung through the small foyer, tossing a passing greeting to the prettily plump little girl at the desk. 'Hi Dimples – now you see to it you have yourself a nice day . . .'

Dimples smiled after the departing bejeaned bottom, before turning back to Blossom. 'Goodness! You've made a quick recovery! Mercedes was telling me you looked like absolute death when you came back from the station with your sister. Where is she now – sleeping off her long journey? I can't wait to see her! Mercedes said that the likeness was – what did she say – was positively, yes that was it, "spinechilling"!' Dimples giggled confidingly and leaned towards Blossom. 'We've had a bet, to tell you the truth. I have bet her a pound that I could tell the difference between the two of you. Mercedes swore to me that she couldn't, not if you were wearing the same clothes.'

Blossom was reluctant to be the cause of Dimples losing a pound, and had already half decided to continue with the deception. After all June would be dead to the world for hours. There was little likelihood of her emerging and spilling the beans. This was the sort of situation which was always happening when they were together, one which Blossom was well used to carrying off with aplomb. She prepared to make her goodbyes, moving towards the potted shoulder-high plant which stood at the front door, when suddenly the small switchboard started buzzing.

Dimples spun round. Blossom waved her hand, she was trying to decide whether to grab the first taxi she saw and go straight to South Molton Street, the first address on June's list of shops, or linger a little along Portobello Road. Though it wasn't a Saturday and therefore there were no stalls for her to browse among, there were plenty of exciting shops and arcades open selling her sort of stuff. It was like being set squarely in Paradise.

The decision was postponed. 'It's for you, June.' Dimples was beckoning, covering the receiver with her short fleshy fingers. How like pigs' trotters they are, Blossom caught herself thinking, I should love to sink my front teeth into those . . .

Dimples nudged her. 'It's Professor Hamilton Hamilton.' She winked. 'He says he's in a callbox so you had better take it here rather than through there where you'd get a little more privacy. I promise I'll block up my ears.' She handed Blossom the telephone and ostentatiously plugged a thumb in each of her ears. Then turned her back. Blossom took the receiver. 'Hello.' She said confidently. 'Professor Hamilton Hamilton?' She must remember to check with June whether she had a pet name for him.

Out in the streets of London Blossom was finding the response of passers-by to be nothing short of amazing. *Everyone* turned around to look at her! It made her feel absolutely *marvellous*! Not of course that she had ever been short of the attention of strangers in her life. As twins she and June had grown used to being stared at, and although singly neither could command that same attention (since nothing could match the curiosity aroused by the sight of duplicate humans), she could always be sure of admiring glances. Certainly from men.

But this was different. Of course the eyes had followed them across Paddington station as the porter had guided them to the taxi-rank. June had looked so chic in her dramatic black and white, with that chocolate biscuit brown on her mouth (which Blossom had borrowed and was now wearing on her own). And she herself had presented a far from conventional picture in her striking poppy-scattered, scarlet satin kimono, with a blazing bunch of artificial flowers, mostly fuschias, secured to the cherry-red scarf around her neck. All, except the scarf, salvaged from the Puddlemouth Amateur Operatic Society's Sale of Goods the previous spring, after their hugely successful production of *Madame Butterfly*. Ouida Pickles of the wool shop had worn this very kimono, splitting it almost in two after the interval, whilst stumbling heavily on stage, three secret Scotches better off. It had taken Blossom less than an hour and a half to stitch it carefully together again, with no sign of the join. She considered it to be one of her finest bargains (not to mention the sweet Sunday session during which she had played a sexy slant-eyed Madame Butterfly to Randolph's dashing Captain Pickering). Yes, between them they had caused quite a minor stir at the station. And as June had explained on the way to her lovely hotel (which was much, much odder and therefore nicer than Blossom had expected), she, June, had after all been on the box the previous evening. And people always loved recognising celebrities in the flesh.

That's what it was, without a doubt – everyone was mistaking her for June! Well it wasn't so surprising, especially in June's white dress and with June's black hat. It had been amusing to see how sure Dimples had been of her identity. The Professor had been equally convinced. 'I beg of you not to interrupt, just listen carefully. I have a plane to catch. I'm in Scotland. I shall meet you tonight at the Gay Hussar – sorry, my dear, but I shall have to leave you to book the table. I suggest nine o'clock, I shan't be able to make it any sooner. Oh, by the way – I have of course missed you desperately . . .' The sound of pips had smothered the rest of his words before the line had gone completely dead.

Blossom paused at the window to look at herself in the massive baroque mirror occupying the central position in an entire display of different mirrors. There must have been at least sixty separate images of herself. She smiled at them all.

'Looks pretty good to me, missus!' A cocky boy, who couldn't have been much older than Pip, paused then passed on whistling. 'Thank you,' Blossom called after his small swaggering body. A ladies' man already, despite his youth.

But she could see what he meant, turning back to her reflections. This dress was French, fashioned from a small amount of crisp cotton piqué into a shaped halter-neck sheath. The strucural engineering enabled her to dispense with her brassiere whilst retaining a succulent, though discreet, amount of cleavage. Smooth brown hills rising from either side of a deep velvety ravine. Her lean strong swimmer's shoulders appeared elegant, even frail, in the cut-away line of the fitted bodice. Blossom raised one elbow, as if to adjust the jaunty peaked cap (the sort worn by umpires at Wimbledon or rather American baseball teams since the peak was decidedly longer). The cap required no adjustment but it had suddenly occurred to Blossom to check on the state of her underarms. There had been no convenient opportunity to shave on the train this morning.

She peered. Not a shadow of stubble in sight.

The sun was climbing in the cloudless sky, Blossom sauntered on in a highly pleasurable state of receptive relaxation. She was keenly aware of that sensation that only cities can give – that at any moment something exciting could happen. The air thrummed with it, with this special expectancy, this vitality, this exuberance and electricity. Perhaps Portobello Road was more alive than most streets and therefore not really representative, but in the mood she was in Blossom felt as high as a steeple. She could have illuminated Piccadilly, have flown over St Pauls, have dived off Putney Bridge and swum all the way to the Port of London with ease.

She suddenly realised that she hadn't had a poke!

Sitting in the taxi on the way to Bond Street (a good choice of shoe shops all around there), Blossom reflected on this fact. She was still reflecting, though her attention had now been diverted by the Marble Arch crowds, when the door of her taxi was unexpectedly wrenched open. The cab had stopped at the lights when Zachary Ram had happened to glance through the window and saw who he took to be June Day. (Rather a co-incidence, that. Only an hour ago he had been enjoying himself drafting a quite beastly and withering review of June Day's current television series for his column in *Views*. He had not yet forgiven her for granting her favours to that senile old goat Hamilton Hamilton, that lunchtime at Stalky's. He knew perfectly well that he should have moved in for the kill just that little bit sooner. But how was he to know that the famed fornicator was breathing down his neck. The knowledge that it was his own fault made the lost opportunity all the more bitter. The harsh review had been simply a self satisfying case of sour grapes, he would have been the first to admit that. He couldn't deny that he still fancied her to madness and would have given anything to have a crack at her cherry. The bitch!)

'Well, well – if it isn't the girl of the moment!'

To both the driver's and Blossom's alarm this male person had now thrown himself headlong into the taxi, slamming the door behind him and sprawled all over the back seat beside Blossom.

The driver, forced to move forward by the traffic on his tail, called back anxiously. 'Are you all right, Miss Day?' He too had recognised his lovely passenger half-way up Bayswater Road. It would be just his luck to have an accident with some fucking lunatic who got turned on by the sight of someone who'd been on the telly. It wasn't his sort if thing, not at all – hadn't he, four years ago, driven Ursula Andress to London Airport, crying all the way, her mascara streaming straight down into her mouth? One person's grief was the same as the next. When you're dead it doesn't matter who you've been. All he wanted was peace. All he needed now was a piss and a pint in a pub. It was near enough to one o'clock, his knocking-off time. The geyser in the back was answering, in the upper class accent overlaid with bastard cockney that these young public school blokes considered to be the way to speak nowadays.

'Don't worry mate – everything's under control back here.' The patronising little sod turned to the girl (who was staring at him as though she had never set eyes on him in her life before). 'Cheer up, June duckie – you surely don't object to giving an old pal a lift do you? I have been waiting for a sodding cab here for nearly twenty minutes . . .' Zachary Ram's voice fell away. He was staring at her now. Christ – she was sexy! At the sight of her swelling breasts, and the slim suntanned legs (crossed in such a way at the knee that a ripe slice of thigh reverberated against his retina) his trouser-worm twerked. It reared up, stallion-style, separating itself from the sticky nest of his nuts. The inside of this taxi was like an inferno! Beads of perspiration began to form along his upper lip. Lord, how he longed to get his teeth around those luscious tits!

And the wide-eyed way she was looking at him ... that mouth, slightly open as if in maidenly amazement ... that tongue. He could see the tongue trembling pinkly between the perfect white teeth. Hadn't he less than two hours ago made some sneering comment about these very teeth in his rough draft? And wasn't he on the way to the *Views'* office at this precise moment in order to polish his final attacking draft and pack it off to press? God-all-fucking-mighty!!! What was wrong with him – had he gone clean round the bend? Or what?

Now the goddess was smiling at him – smiling at *him*! With an expression in those great eyes that he had never had directed towards him from a woman or a girl for all the years he had been fucking (which actually was not that many). It was blinding, that green gaze of hers. The lust pounded along his loins, had he been just several years younger he'd be close to shooting off by now. He could almost swear that he could *smell* her, his nostrils full of her creamy cunt. That pungent mixture of fish (the fruit of the sea) and the ripest of all the rich cheeses ...

'Whew!' He stretched his short thick legs, suddenly conscious of the fact that if they stood side by side, she would be at least a foot taller. But so what – be at just the right height to clamp his mouth on her mammaries ... whew, but dare he say it ... dare he suggest that she and he might ...

The taxi slowed down and then swung around the sharp swerve of New Bond Street. Shit! She was preparing to get out, he was going to lose her again. He couldn't let her go this time without even getting her telephone number ...

'Oh. Haven't you got it already?' she had replied to his request. But her tender look of surprise had turned his stomach to liquid. She'd been half out of the cab by this time and had turned to him, one foot already on the kerb. He could see almost up to her pussy from this position and had to gulp hard to restrain himself from stretching his fingers to touch the inside edge of her panties. His spirits and hopes were plummeting each second. The taxi was revving, impatient to be off. She gave him her number, reeling it off without thinking, as if she gave it out three hundred times a day — which she most likely did. He could feel his face setting in lines of utmost despondency.

And then she kissed him.

It wasn't quite on the lips, but it was near enough. Realising at that last heart-stopping moment that a kiss was on the way, he had engineered to have his mouth (all of it) at the appropriate place.

She had actually been aiming, he knew, at his cheek.

But arriving at the junction of Fleet Street and Chancery Lane, paying off the taxi, mounting the office stairs towards his working lunch hour; sitting down at his typewriter to reword an entirely new review of June Day's television series — he could still taste her kiss on his tongue.

June was no better and, though she was no worse, Blossom could tell that this was a twenty-four-hour thing. The only way to combat the virulence of the bug was to sweat it out in bed. She ran herself a bathful of hot water, using June's bathroom instead of her own next door in order to make the start of the evening more companionable. June was drowsy and drugged from the combination of cold cures that Blossom saw fit to administer. She was sipping her second hot whisky-and-honey, but not enjoying it as much as she would have done had she been well. Her throat was still sore despite repeated garglings with guaranteed remedies that Blossom had bought in Boots. The hot whisky-and-honey now tasted unpleasantly of Listerine, and far from soothing her throat seemed to be setting it painfully on fire. The only advantage as far as June could tell was that it did heighten her whirling sense of unreality. Today her infrequent waking hours were merely a dreamy extension of the vivid fantasy world she inhabited whilst asleep. She was looking forward to re-entering that world as quickly as possible — as soon as she could groggily urge the ebullient Blossom to hit the road.

It had already been decided between them that Blossom should avail herself of June's dinner invitation from Professor Hamilton Hamilton. The question was, how should she spend her time until then? There were various alternatives – to Blossom's amazement.

'You mean this is how it is every single evening of the week – all these invites to choose from!' she had gasped excitedly.

June had closed her heavy lids, lined as they seemed with sandpaper. The last thing she could bear to think about was the frenzied supply of socialising at her disposal – all that smiling! All that shoulder-hugging, that hand-shaking, that cheek-kissing! That arse-licking! All that absolutely artificial intimacy . . .

She raked through the scattered cards on her bedspread. These were the formal invitations to functions which had been prearranged weeks, even months, before. They had been addressed to her personally at Television Tower and so had been dealt with by the secretary she had been given for the duration of the series. If she went on to make another set of programmes for the same company, then she would be designated a permanent secretary of her own, but the company were trying very hard to sign June up with a five-year contract, a move which Cherie was adamant that they should resist. It certainly would not be worth tying herself up for anything like that long for the sake of having a secretary to handle among other things, her increasingly overwhelming social diary. Even though things seemed to be getting out of hand!

'Blimey!' Blossom was carried away in a schoolgirl delirium. Of course they received invitation cards at home. Scrawled scraps of cardboard, the back of the corn-flake packet, with 'bring a bottle' on the bottom, shoved through the letter-box by Emily Shawl from time to time. Rather awful abstract lino-cuts, depicting God knows what, beneath a desperate plea to visit somebody's studio . . . 'wine and cheese'. Larger events of this nature (and after all many of their friends were highly respected artists who entertained in most civilised Bohemian style), were simply arranged over the phone. More often than not on the spur of the moment, but certainly with no more than a week's notice. Even so, these get-togethers, these lengthy and boisterous Bacchanalian occasions were rarer than Blossom would have liked. She actually *adored* going out. Dolling herself up. Being admired and behaving in a deliberately (though innocently) flirtatious manner. It was her idea of real enjoyment. She had always regretted the fact that marrying so young

84

and having had the children straight away meant she had missed out on the chance of being a real good-time girl. There was something vacuous in her nature that made her ideal for the role.

But a thought occurred to her now. 'Who am I going as — you or me?' She studied those invitation cards in her hand. A Private View of the Surrealist Artist, Liberty Bean. Dame Tiger Oats, that wonderful old girl that June had interviewed about six months ago, had spoken of Liberty Bean and her work. Blossom would have liked to have seen it tonight. But she was also keen to see the one-act sexual farce at Shepherds Bush (all girls and a bowlful of goldfish), which started at seven-thirty and was all over in an hour. That would give her time to get over to Soho in time to meet the Professor. Similarly she felt drawn to attend the pre-dinner drinks ('trust you will dine too, June dear!') at the Barbican apartment of Hilda Vengeance. The barrister, the gay one, that June had met first at the Female Conference. Apart from Emily Shawl and Pots, Blossom had never really been in a totally lesbian environment. She felt that it might be rather her milieu and she liked the sound of this witty woman lawyer, Hilda Vengeance. At the same time she was reluctant not to put in an appearance at the party being thrown to coincide with the re-release of the Belle Nuddle Albums from the '50s, or the Champagne Reception for Bethlehem Bungalows at the Savoy ('A SNAZZY SARONG SWIMSUIT FOR EACH OF THE LADIES!!') She rather fancied a free Sarong swimsuit as a change from the eternal bikini. The motivation was rather stronger than vanity, she just liked the idea of getting something for nothing.

But these were only a sample of the avenues open to Blossom between now and nine o'clock. With the Professor she knew that she would be perfectly all right. She had met him before and she was able to handle any situation whether she pretended to be her sister, or simply presented herself as who she was. Either way he would be delighted. This was not so with these other functions. If June had been well enough to go to any single one of them, taking Blossom as her twin, the success of the evening would have been assured. If she went on her own, as herself, then it was doubtful whether her first few hours out on the town would be anything more than a miserably damp squib. After all who would want to meet her?

Down in Cornwall this situation didn't arise. There she was known and revered as being the wife of Randolph Tree. She was a respected and admired parent in the community, the mother of Willow and Pip. She was an indulged and highly popular bundle of fun; an amusingly dressed, faintly eccentric, shamelessly sexy, unfailingly attractive and warm animal – who, when on form, could coax the conviction from the chilliest critic that here was a sensational flamboyant beauty.

This evening she felt a little in her magic mood. It had started with that friend of June's, that poor pimply besotted boy in the taxi. The youth that June had denied as being a friend of hers at all.

'But he's an absolute toad!' she had exclaimed when Blossom had given a detailed description of her taxi intruder. 'Everyone *hates* him! He *crucifies* programmes in his ghastly column. And he writes it so well – so viciously, but cleverly, that everyone reads him. You've read him, I'm sure. Zachary Ram. He has taken over as TV critic of *Views*. Randy will know his stuff, he's very much one of the new young bright boys.'

'Zachary Ram – was *that* Zachary Ram. I have read him. So's Randy. He holds him in very high esteem.'

'That's the trouble, everyone does you see. We're all rather dreading what he'll write about the programme. He loathes me, I do know that . . .' June pulled a long painful face.

'I'm sure that he doesn't loathe you.' Blossom gave a girlish giggle. She was feeling not displeased with herself.

'Oh yes he does! I assure you we've barely exchanged more than a few words.'

'He won't loathe you after this morning. This morning you kissed him. He nearly wet himself, little love . . .'

'This morning *I* did what! Blossom – what have you been doing?'

Blossom giggled again with full-throated satisfaction. 'I have been going around kissing television critics leading them to believe that all along it is you. I shouldn't concern yourself for one moment over the *Views* review – I should think that he will write something absolutely smashing.'

Blossom went (as June) to the Belle Nuddle Album launch since it was at Notting Hill Gate and on her way to the girls and goldfish farce at Shepherds Bush. She had settled on these two as being the safest events, with less likelihood of having to commit herself in any form of intense conversation. This was a testing time after all, and she was being thrown in at the deep end of London social life. After ten minutes of the Belle Nuddle launch she could see that there was nothing to worry about at all. All she had to do was stand there with a drink in her hand, a smile on her face and an expression of concentrated listening aimed at whoever was talking to her. No one, absolutely no one, was interested in what *she* had to say. June had warned her, trying to be reassuring that this would be the case. 'They are all much too busy with their own giant egos to be bothered about you and yours. Why do you think I've done so well as an interviewer – only because I am such a bloody good listener. You could do my job, Blossom, just as well as me – no, honestly you could! You go there tonight and see what I mean. Only,' June raised a weak warning wrist, 'Kid, do be careful who you kiss on my behalf . . .'

There would have been plenty to kiss (on her own behalf, bugger June's!) if she had felt so inclined. But Randolph had rung as she had been about to leave, and his dear, sweet voice was still warm in her ears. Even so, she felt dangerously randy. In the distance she could see (she could swear it was him) Rod Stewart. And further along the same side of the crowded room was Paul McCartney with Linda, his wife. She could imagine telling Willow and Pip all about this. Randy wouldn't have been particularly impressed, pop was hardly his scene. Probably the kids wouldn't either, come to think of it. They had idols of their own. She took another drink from the tray being offered to her. The first of the day, well actually this was now the third since she had been here. She glanced at her watch and saw with no real feeling of regret that there was no time left for the girls and goldfish after all. She had been coasting so well here that there had been no such thing as time. Her first hurdle and she'd passed with flying colours!

She told the taxi to wait for her outside the Savoy, she would be in there no more than five minutes – she promised. June had claimed that was the only sort of appearance she would need to put in at the Bethlehem Bungalows in order to claim her Sarong Swimsuit. 'Honestly Bloss, you won't like it when you get it. I can just imagine what it will be like – absolutely ghastly, all covered in palm trees with a skirt on the crossover and ruching down the side . . .'

But Blossom had been entranced. 'Sort of '40s, do you mean? Oh, Randy will love that – I shall be able to do my Betty Grable number, I've got some marvellous white wedgies already to go with it!' She was determined not to miss the Sarong Swimsuit.

It took less than five minutes. A dazzling blonde receptionist at the entrance to the drawing room of Suite 244 (hired by Bethlehem Bungalows for the evening) was handing our prettily packaged swimsuits to each female arrival. She herself was wearing one, a completely bumless design with simply a string passing between the division of the buttocks to join the three strategically placed postage stamps on the front of the body. The stamps bearing the head of Her Majesty, appeared to be made of cleverly printed cotton, but with a form of adhesive backing. Each stayed perfectly in position as the blonde moved, and although the strings looped one to the other and linked round at the back, they were simply a brightly coloured device to lead the eye all over the torso.

'Colour preference, darling?' the blonde gushed at Blossom. Beyond her, in the main mass of the reception Blossom spotted at least three or four other blondes similarly attired. There were many, many men in the room. Beside their sober business suits the blondes' virtually nude bodies looked obscene. Though each girl looked as though she was having a hell of a good time, and presumably was being paid a decent whack on an hourly rate, there was something distinctly depressing about the whole set-up. Seedy. That was the word. Suddenly Blossom felt the urge to get away.

'What shade do you fancy? There's turquoise, those are the 1/2p stamps. There's blue, those are the 9p; green, they're the 2p.' The blonde's radiant smile rooted Blossom to the spot. She wouldn't be allowed to leave until she had made her choice.

'Great gimmick, isn't it! Sure you can't stop longer for a nice little drinkie? Can't we tempt you to a glass of the bubbly – no? Shame.'

Blossom stumbled gratefully into the waiting taxi clutching a whole pile of literature on the construction, durability and desirability of Bethlehem Bungalows. A thick folder of pamphlets, expensively illustrated throughout with photographs of building sites in every single stage of development from the laying of foundations to the final stage – to the drinks being served on the completed patio. The girl in the photograph of this idyllic scene was not, Blossom noted, wearing a Sarong Swimsuit, but a perfectly straightforward Marks and Spencer bikini. Blossom recognised the one, there had been hundreds the very same on the beaches of Puddlemouth this summer. Blossom fingered her tiny ribboned envelope containing the tethered stamps. She had chosen turquoise in the end, a favourite colour of Randy's. Well – at least he would enjoy her new swimsuit.

There was just time, if she stayed no longer than twenty minutes, to put in an appearance at the Barbican apartment of Hilda Vengeance. Although June had warned her against pretending to be June. 'In the mood you're in, I can imagine the repercussions. If you go there, you go as yourself – please Bloss . . .'

Blossom had promised faithfully.

But now, driving up to the brooding nest of buildings – so out of character with the rest of the city, Blossom wasn't sure. The trouble was now that she no longer felt like herself. She had grown rather used to being June. To being treated as a successful career girl rather than a Cornish housewife. She didn't wish to admit to her own identity any longer. She no longer felt that it was something of which she could justifiably feel proud. It was the first time in her entire life that this thought had even occurred to her.

'Have I got time do you think,' Blossom consulted the taxi-driver, 'to visit this friend of mine in the Barbican, just for about twenty minutes – then go on to The Sliced Eye Gallery in Soho, for whatever time I have left – so that I could still be at The Gay Hussar restaurant, in Greek Street by nine o'clock?'

'Blimey! You up from the country or summit? Just like the bleedin' Yanks! They always try and cram in the impossible too . . .'

But it wasn't impossible. Strolling, entranced, through the streets of Soho which lay between The Sliced Eye and The Gay Hussar, Blossom mused on how little the British actually stretched themselves. There she was with three minutes in hand, having done every single thing that she had set out to do (except the girls and the goldfish). And what's more she had so far absolutely sailed through the evening! Well, almost.

There had been one or two sticky moments. On her arrival at Hilda Vengeance's she had been uncertain which of the ladies present was the hostess. She had quite wrongly conjured up the image of a tall, handsome woman with a strong nose, a determined chin and a firm, well-defined set of sculptured lips. Dressed (Blossom couldn't imagine why she thought this) in a man's hacking jacket with a gent's shirt and tie, and a thick Harris tweed skirt above thick ribbed stockings and a pair of hefty brogues.

Not a single person in the ultra-modern setting of the room remotely fitted this description.

Hilda turned out to be a rather short, busty Jewess with a tiny waist, trim ankles and remarkable doe-eyes, reminiscent of Bambi, above a pertly retroussé nose. Her appearance was completely at odds with her personality, which was more American than British. More New York than the City of London. She delivered everything she said in the way that an actress would. One actress in particular sprang to Blossom's mind – Coral Browne (who several years ago had married one of Blossom's favourite screen actors – the velvet-voiced Vincent Price). But the dry irony was close to the wit of Dorothy Parker. To Blossom's great delight she swore like a seaman.

But Hilda's appearance had taken her by surprise – it was so unlike what she had been expecting. June had not given a description of Hilda at any time during their discussion of where Blossom might be calling in this evening. At that time they hadn't thought that there would really be an opportunity to fit Hilda in. Also Blossom had been put off the idea of her promise to go as herself. Why had she (and June) always had such difficulty in sticking to promises – hadn't they at one time promised each other never ever to make another promise, at least to each other . . .

Hilda had been occupied at the other side of the room when Blossom had made her entrance. The first impression Blossom had was of a roomful of perfectly normal-looking females. Middle class women and girls, the usual mixture of jeans, kaftans, straightforward shirtwaisters. Nothing untoward, no big hulks, not a single butch bitch amongst them! Blossom felt ever so slightly let down, though wouldn't have wished to admit it – not to display her bigotted ignorance and preconceptions to the world. But it was perfectly true that deep inside her she had been rather imagining that she was going to walk right into the party and be instantly *raped*. Dumped down in the middle of the proceedings and pleasured by an enormous baby pink dildo.

Brutally. With stormy eyed, massive thighed, Amazon girls pressing their hard bodies to hers.

That's how she had imagined it.

She was in the middle of a discussion with a woman gynaecologist and a PT Instructress in the Womens Auxiliary Corps when Hilda Vengeance had first addressed her. 'Well,' Hilda had said, an amused twist to her red lips. 'No special greeting for the hostess yet, I notice!'

Blossom froze. Then she looked around. 'I don't seem to see her around.'

Hilda caught her by the waist and hugged her tightly against the firmly upholstered bosom. 'You're an absolute doll – but don't overdo it! I haven't lost that much. Only a bloody stone. But not fading away quite yet –'. The tricky moment had passed! But at The Sliced Eye Gallery several potentially dangerous situations of a similar nature had occurred. The greatest hazard of being June was the not knowing which amongst these gatherings of strangers were friends and familiars, and which people June had never set eyes on before.

The only way out for Blossom, the only practical solution was just to smile indiscriminately at everyone. It proved to be a wonderful way of meeting people, but it presented the problem that she never got to know anyone's name.

'You two know each other I'm sure.' Blossom lost count of how many times she was forced into this trick as a means of introducing people to each other, without the advantage of knowing the names of either. It was a social device that she had learned to adopt with great success over the years when her memory failed to supply a name to match the familiar face with whom she might have happened to be in conversation. The two persons would wait, gazing first at each other then shaking their heads. 'No, haven't had the pleasure . . .' 'No, can't say we have met . . .' Then they would turn enquiringly toward Blossom, waiting for her to effect proper introductions. To which she would smilingly insist: 'But I could have *sworn* that you had met!' Then, only then would she learn what they were called. 'I'm so-and-so.' 'I'm such-and-such. Nice to meet you.' Etcetera, etcetera.

That got her out of a few spots.

What surprised her most was how few people posed her the real questions that she had been dreading. That is, genuinely serious and searching demands to be told about her work. It was as if, she reflected (now almost at the Gay Hussar), she had already proved herself as an intelligent and capable woman. But more than that – as a *success* in this fiercely competitive stratum of London life. Having done so there was no longer any need to strive to impress. The mere fact of being sufficiently "in" to be invited, that was enough in itself. She was simply yet another in a gathering of celebrities . . . The question now, still undecided in her mind, was who should she be with Professor Hamilton Hamilton? And that question required an immediate answer – she had arrived at the scarlet door of The Gay Hussar. One half-minute late. A woman's prerogative. As soon as she set eyes on the Professor there was no doubt in her mind. She knew without question who she should be.

CHAPTER THREE

'Blossom, are you busy – I'd like a hand with this –' Randolph Tree grinned wickedly to himself. He was standing at the top of the stairs, his erect cock sticking straight out of his winter-weight combinations (the pale colour of porridge) and the sturdy corduroy trousers which he would wear right through till the first signs of spring.

June was in the middle of making her mincemeat for the Christmas mincepies, and had just got to the stage of mixing the shredded suet in with the brown sugar and spice, the dried fruits, walnuts and chopped apples. She was looking forward to adding the brandy (and taking a hefty swig from the bottle). 'Oh, darling – can't it wait, whatever it is?' she shouted back. 'Only I'm just coming to the brandy –'

'Bring the brandy with you! This won't take very long, I promise. I could do it on my own but with your help I'd make a better job of it.'

'Hold on –' June went to swill her hands at the kitchen sink.

'I'm holding!' Randolph grasped his shaft like a truncheon, standing perfectly still like a statue so that this would be the first sight to greet his wife as she rounded the bend of the stair. He composed his features into the sort of noble expression that ruling monarchs or valiant warriors display on coins. And with the thick dark beard which he had grown since the summer he actually did look the part.

June hummed as she dried her hands. She loved Randy's interruptions, but they were becoming so frequent lately that she couldn't imagine how on earth he managed to get any work of his own done at all. Yesterday, for instance, he had spent the *entire* day in her company. Not letting her out of his sight for a single second – not even to go to the lavatory. 'I'm insane about the smell of your shit!' he had suddenly an-nounced, sitting on the edge of the black-enamelled bath (a bad mistake of Blossom's – the black bathroom. A bloody nightmare with white talc), watching her strain. And then he'd pleaded, 'Please, please will you let me wipe your botty, Blossom – I promise I'll do it most beautifully.' And he had. As skilfully and as tenderly as a nurse would have done. June had paid him for that as well as for the following poke. They agreed between them that it came under the category of imaginative foreplay.

Before leaving the kitchen area of this the ground floor, June checked the contents of her oven. She had a spiced date crumble pudding in there for Pip and Willow's tea. It had roughly three-quarters of an hour to go, by which time they would be home from school. She was also roasting a half leg of pork in preparation for the cold buffet she would be serving tomorrow evening. There would be about ten guests – no, more than that. All the darts team anyway were coming for a practice session upstairs in Randy's study. (Bloss hadn't believed that when June had told her on the phone. 'But no one is *ever* allowed into the sanctuary, not even me!')

'Oh, *I've* been in there,' June said smugly.

'Bloody good for you too!' Blossom had responded warmly. There was no rivalry between them.

The rind of the boned half-leg of pork had been removed. It lay succulently in a roasting pan at the bottom of the oven, tied into a fat sausage shape, surrounded by the trimmings, the skin cut into strips, and a pig's foot split in two. The added water came halfway up the pan. June had made two rows of incisions along the meat, into which she had pressed chopped fresh herbs and little spikes of garlic, rolled in pepper and salt. The next day, after removing the cooked meat (later this afternoon) and straining the liquid into a bowl, she would carve the cold pork into thin slices. Then she would turn out the jellied stock, chop it finely and arrange around the meat, serving it with a potato salad.

But before that she would have warmed the cockles of their hearts with her hot chestnut cream soup, a recipe she had tried and tested on Emily Shawl only last week. She must remember to make a supply for the deep freeze – or not, there were many other planned dishes in her mind for the deep freeze. It was strange how easily she'd adapted to her new role.

Randy was calling again, he sounded impatient. But she

94

couldn't help it she simply *had* to take one last look at her seascape. She had put what she considered to be the finishing touches to the tiny canvas just over an hour ago. And so far nobody had seen it but herself. It was very, very good.

She had painted seven of these seascapes in the last nine weeks, taking just over a week to complete each of them. But her plan was to finish a whole set, a full dozen, and then to mount them as one on a large prepared square of backed and reinforced board. It would represent her personal and changing view of the pounding ocean outside her window.

This communal room, the open-plan cooking area at the other end, was where she had chosen to set up her easel. Here at the indoor side of the balcony, an area now strictly forbidden to the rest of the family.

Not that the rest of the family viewed her artistic efforts with anything other than proud and affectionate respect.

'It sort of looks like a bowl of washing-up water, doesn't it?' Pip had said ruminatively about the first painting, his head on one side.

'Oh, thanks very much, son!' June had tugged his short hair.

'No, Mum —' Willow had put loving arms around her waist. 'He doesn't mean it rudely. I know what he means. It's all the swirls. Isn't that the sort of effect that you were after?'

'Yes, it is. You're quite right.' June had smiled to reassure them both. She continued to be astonished at what very clever, kind and considerate children, her sister's children had turned out to be. Of course she had known they were *nice* and she'd known them since birth, it wasn't as if they were strangers. But that was hardly the same as living with them day in and day out — as their mother. Or rather with them believing her to be their mother. In fact the children had been more the cause for doubt in her mind that the life-switch would work, more even than Randolph.

'The kids will *know* though, Blossom, that it's me and not you . . .' This had been at the start of the thrilling laying of their plans. When the idea of the swap was still partly a fantasy in their minds. But even then they had begun to practise as though rehearsing for the eventual reversal of roles.

'How will they *know*? You mean that you think children have some extra-sensory perception as to whether or not someone is their natural mother?' Blossom had snorted rudely through the end of her nose. 'Bollocks! They've researched it with little mon-keys – taken the mother away and replaced her with an old bol-ster wrapped round a hot water bottle. And nobody has been able to tell the difference – honestly, I've seen a programme on television . . .'

June had interrupted. 'Bollocks to you too, Bloss! The facts remain that Pip and Willow are not little monkeys –'

'Ooh, you should see them sometimes!'

June continued '– and nor am I an old bolster with supplied inner warmth. Those two are very bright eleven and twelve-year-olds, who would spot the difference in one second flat. I just know that they would, I'm worried. I'd love to try it for a lark but I don't think I could fool them.'

'You're quite wrong. You could. The reason's quite simple. They're absolutely wrapped up in a complete world of their own – honestly. Do you want a run-down of their day? Well, I shall give it to you – and I promise you that you'll be amazed at how very little we see of each other, the kids and me. We hardly ever eat together, for a start. They have breakfast on their own. I lay it all ready the night before. Cornflakes. Bananas, or apples and oranges. Sliced bread ready for toasting, which they love doing themselves. Butter, or Flora (easier to spread straight from the fridge), honey or jam, milk. Instant coffee, sometimes they prefer teabags. Everything's there. What you don't understand is that they prefer to be self-sufficient. They have their mid-day meal at school. In the evening they tear in, throw down their stomachs whatever happens to be there – I usually just leave cheese or cold chicken, or ham. Something like that, with a bowl of tomatoes and lettuce, celery, radishes – whatever's in season. You'll be going into the winter so they will need something warmer. In which case you leave a shepherds pie in the oven, or a cauliflower cheese, or a steak and kidney pie – just something simple, they don't care. Sometimes I only know that they've been back because the food has gone. Yes, really! They spend the whole time out with their pals, or lolling in front of the television – it's OK, you don't have to put up with them in front of our colour telly. We've bought them a new one of their own which they have on their own floor beneath the rest of the house. I can envisage the day when we shall have to devise a way that they even have their own entrance to the house – knock a hole in the outside wall, something like that. Randy's all for the little buggers having as independent a life as possible from us. He says that apart from the creature comforts of food, warmth and clean clothes all the children need to know is that we are there if and when they need us. And that's about how it is at the moment.'

June had not been convinced. 'What about when they're ill?'

'When they are ill, they just stay in bed. They try it on when they have exams at school. You'll learn to tell the difference. And if you think it's anything serious, you get the doctor round. It's a new one by the way –'

'Has old Wisdom died? You didn't tell me.' June had stared accusingly at Blossom. 'There you are you see – there are all these sort of things that I should obviously know. I would give myself away left, right and centre.'

'Not if we go into everything thoroughly. It's a straightforward research job, no more involved than that. The sort of thing that Espionage is up to all the time.' Blossom had smiled reassuringly and had hugged her sister tight. 'Honestly, baby, your part of it is going to be miles easier than mine. You do at least know my life and all the people in it – it's a pretty small circle, after all. And nothing much happens most of the time.'

June replied nervously. 'But that's just the trouble. It's just in a small intimate set-up like yours that anything untoward is going to be immediately noticed. The very familiarity will make the slightest strangeness on my part seem even odder.'

Blossom had shaken her head most emphatically. 'It's a community of oddities, you know that. Small eccentricities are not only expected but welcomed as tiny diversions with which to pass the day. Half the time people you may have had dinner with the night before will not even greet you in the street – it means they're involved in their work. No more than that. They're bound up in the creative process, just thinking. That's why Randy likes living there so much. He can behave as he chooses and no one regards him with awe. He happens to be a famous philosopher, but so what – in Puddlemouth that's no more special than being a painter or a fisherman. You could return tomorrow as me and behave in any way you like, be completely withdrawn until you felt surer of yourself – even with the kids and with Randy. Everyone would accept it as natural behaviour. They would, honestly. They'd just think that London had had its effect on you, that you were feeling unsettled and that it would take you a little time to acclimatize yourself to being back home.'

This indeed was precisely what had happened. Walking slowly up the stairs now to be confronted (any second) by Randolph's exposed privates, June reflected on the events of the momentous past four months. Momentous to her because the change had been so fundamental, though no more fundamental than it had been for Blossom. The fabulously fortunate thing, they agreed between them, was how successfully they had coped with the switch, themselves. How tragic if one of them had taken to her new life as to the manner born, loving every single minute of it, waking each morning with the secret knowledge that for yet another day she would be who she was not, getting away with it yet again – whilst the other was already bitterly regretting it. And worse, wanting their roles to revert back to normal.

But this had not happened – so far. And if the likelihood appeared to be even remotely looming up in the darkest recesses of the minds of either, it was understood that the dreaded words should be spoken. In truth, neither girl could really believe her good fortune. At the start of the experiment, during those first hazardous weeks in August when the prearranged daily phone calls were quite obviously not enough to cover the incidences of the unexpected, each dreaded that the other might admit to thinking that they had made a mistake. That the joke had gone far enough. That they had had their fun, but now it was time to call it a day. But their mutual reassurances were absolutely genuine, they came jointly and independently to the joyful conclusion that in having changed over at this point in their lives, they were without doubt experiencing the best of both worlds.

'You are *sure* Bloss, you're not regretting it?'

'June, I am *absolutely* sure!'

'You're not . . .' June had hesitated before putting into words what she felt certain to be the case. 'You're not missing Randy too much?' She had held her breath through the small pause before Blossom's reply.

'Missing him – *of course* I'm missing him, silly! But you're there taking good care of him for me so it's all in the family. How are the games going, by the way?'

June had laughed in relief. 'The games? Oh well, we've got a new thing – now I pay him. He does it all. I hardly do anything anymore!' Blossom had been intrigued by this development between her husband and sister. Throughout her entire married life she had always been the one to make the first sexual move, until it would have seemed vaguely obscene had it been the other way around. It wasn't that Randolph had become sexually lazy, but that she enjoyed the ritual of seduction so much. She relished the power to arouse him sexually. It delighted her to feel that she was in control of their games. Although their financial arrangement, whereby she charged him for each intimate act, had originally developed from the amusing idea that this might be a novel way of providing her with the housekeeping money and her dress allowance, this money bond helped the illusion that she was the one who had the upper hand. True, she was an object, but this way an object only available at a certain price. The price being dependent on just how much effort and imagination she chose to throw into each performance. Once, when tired and rather irritable, her periods approaching, she had set an arbitrary figure of 50p on the deal. Her intention being simply to slip down her tights (one leg out was enough) and sprawl back passively on the settee in front of the television. And yet, curiously, there must have been an element of the erotic in her weary lethargy which had sparked off an unparalleled passion in her partner. So much so that he had ripped the remainder of her clothing from her limbs, flinging himself forcefully between her brutally wrenched thighs and covering her neck with such livid love-bites that she had been forced into scarves for a week.

It had been an eye-opener.

Even so it had never occurred to her to reverse their sexual roles. Certainly not to the point where she would be paying him! And yet, why not! The more Blossom thought about it the more she applauded June for this revolutionary approach. Now it was the turn of Randolph to provide the sexual surprises, to wrack his brains for ways and means of titillating the sensual appetite of his wife. And knowing Randy as she did, Blossom didn't doubt for a moment that it was the sort of challenge that he would enjoy. He would be in a position to consult his considerable bibliography on the subject. His sexual section extended, as far as she could remember, across seven shelves of the library in his study. At one time this had been their favourite bedtime reading, with the advantages of practical application of newly discovered techniques immediately to hand. But of late, this pleasant practice had fallen by the way. Replaced by other seductions. Late night brandy. Bournvita. The undemanding bathos of end of the evening television. Or else, in his case, indigestible philosophical tomes. Or in her's, the latest well-reviewed novel.

It had arrived at the point, she could see now reviewing the situation from this distance, where their sex-life was really her responsibility. Like the cooking, and the shopping and the cleaning. And although it had never been anything short of idyllically successful (hadn't she, Blossom, devoted every waking moment to the pursuit!), perhaps a radical change of approach could bring nothing but a beneficial breath of fresh air. She only hoped that dear sweet Randolph felt this to be so.

Randolph did.

He had missed Blossom more than he had believed it possible to miss anyone. He pined for her as keenly as if she had died. She had been away from him for exactly two weeks, three days and five and three-quarter hours. Not counting the fifteen-minute delay in the arrival of her train. And yet, although his sense of loneliness had been so absolute that he had done what he vowed he wouldn't do – that is start pestering her with telephone calls – he had hidden his pain. The parting, after all, had been at his instigation. She needed a break, a change, and he had rather welcomed it himself. But the reality, by the end of the first day, had become unbearable. And worse at the end of the long, dream-logged night, threshing about in their vast four-poster bed. Feeling in vain for her smooth supple haunch, for the handful of breast to cling on to. In the morning, he had rung again in utter anguish, simply to hear her voice. And as unrecognisable though it was (the devilish misfortune to catch some miserable flu bug) it had been an enormous relief. So much so that this had become the pattern throughout the remainder of her visit.

He didn't find it strange that the girls had decided not to leave London after all. It had given Blossom a chance to wander around the shops, to visit exhibitions, the theatre, see films, eat at restaurants (even dance at one nightclub!). All things and places that in Puddlemouth she could only read about. He was well aware that Blossom had a butterfly side to her nature which responded to the less cerebral side of life. It was only right that she should be allowed – no, not allowed – allowed was altogether too much as if he were her keeper and she his possession, his little girl, his toy. She was his wife. She was his partner. She was his equal, his other half. And without her he ceased to exist as a whole.

After the first three nights on his own, his sexual frustration was making him shiver in bed. It was August and he felt deathly cold. At six in the morning he was driven to run a bath and for the first time in so many years that he couldn't remember the last time, he masturbated. It brought him no mental relief whatsoever. He watched the thin milky substance spurt from his cock, still grasping the shaft firmly in his fist. The all-black bathroom was lined with mirror tiles. Randolph was surrounded by images of himself. Cock-in-hand. He looked strained and unhappy like an adolescent boy caught in the act. He looked guilty and not a little mad. The next time he wanked (the following evening) it was in bed, with the electric blanket for warmth and an absolutely appalling programme on the television. One which he and Blossom had even forbidden to the children – an American detective series of unparalleled puerility. But it was summer and there was nothing else better. He enjoyed it hugely, and what was more he lapped up a similar diet of pap for the rest of the evening. To his surprise he found that he had gone to bed at seven-thirty! At ten past ten, unable to stay awake any longer in this unendurable state of isolation, he tossed off at a frantic speed into a pair of Blossom's gossamer panties, then put out the light before falling asleep.

He slept an inordinate amount. Like a teenager, like a person unable to cope with the traumas of life, he sought refuge in sleep. By the first weekend with still ten more days to go before Blossom's return, Randolph was sure that he was suffering a minor breakdown. His behaviour had shaken him – not with alarm. After all he was a great thinker, one who had made a study of the human animal and the human reaction to enforced conditions, including stress. No, it wasn't alarm that he felt. But he was intrigued, he was surprised. His interest had been deeply aroused and was leading him towards an entirely new concept regarding the sexuality of man. His own behaviour, so out of character, would serve as the germination of necessary extensive research in the future. Blossom's absence had proved valuable to his work after all!

He began to take notes. He recorded the desperation of the dawn masturbation, the swift pleasure of the despoiling of Blossom's gossamer panties. And then he recorded the rest. The morning after the despoiling he had awoken with an erection whilst conscious of needing to pee. The erection subsided as he relieved himself, as he would expect it to. The hour was early, if he got up now there would be a further hour or so to wait before the light broke over the sea and the skies. But he found himself lacking his usual enthusiasm for the sight. His normal procedure of rising at dawn now appeared rather perverse without Blossom to return to at eight or thereabouts for their morning fuck – thence to proceed downstairs for breakfast (or the other way around, if she felt like it). He felt disorientated, as badly as any person of firm habit whose normal programming has been turned upside down.

And so he returned to his bed.

The first sight that caught his eye was that of Blossom's spunky drawers. They lay pink and crumpled against the black sheet, a delicate reminder of their delicious owner. And of the purpose to which he had put them last night.

He fell on them with a groan and stuffed them to his mouth, kissing their sweet and faintly perfumed crotch. Sniffing them like a dog, rubbing them roughly all over his face, hugging them against his slack cock and balls. And then he bent down and pulled them on.

The effect was grotesque yet at the same time mesmerising. It was something to do with the contrast, the contrast of his muscled and rather hairy masculine flesh against the fine cobwebbed texture of the feminine garment. The sight seemed to contradict itself, it looked all wrong. But only, as Randolph later wrote in the appendix to his notes, because of a mental conditioning. It only looked odd and faintly obscene (also frankly perverse) because this was not the apparel one would normally expect to find on the body of a full-grown healthy man in this day and age. Apart from that, there was no viable reason why he, on studying his reflection in the mirrored ceiling of the four-poster (there must be an interesting explanation of Blossom's need to surround herself with mirrors – to do with being a twin and needing constantly to relate to her double?), should

102

experience quite such a shock. Nor why, secondary to that shock and following hard on its heels, he should be aware of a growing excitement. Not even a specifically sexual excitement either, as yet. But an eerier and less familiar sensation, as if he were removed from the person reflected above him in the mirror. As if that person were being watched by an interested observer, a stranger, but one whose impartiality and distance was mutely denied by the expression of intense concentration contorting the twisted features.

His hand slid slowly down to the triangle of flimsy fabric barely covering his cock or his balls. Blossom's knickers, as he would have expected, were far too brief to begin to fit. His bollocks bulged out, one each side of the narrow crotch. Whilst his still inert penis, in no sense extended (yet) lay pressed hard against his belly, the tip peeping out from beneath the line of the waist-elastic like the nose of an inquisitive puppy. And the constriction of his genitals was in no way unpleasant. Randolph even enjoyed it – it reminded him of Blossom and the way she had sometimes of squeezing him down there, cupping him tightly in both hands and whispering low threats.

At the memory his genitals jumped.

That evening he retired to his bedroom as early as the night before, around seven-thirty. Only this time he didn't retire to bed. Instead he stripped off, poured himself a large Scotch, adding a liberal supply of ice-cubes from the small bedside fridge (there solely for this purpose). Then he stood at the window watching the last of the summer visitors straggle off the beach below. He was wondering what to put on.

All day he had been like this, in a skin-tingling state of aroused excitement. As if he had stumbled upon a delicious secret, a forbidden activity, a subversive way of life. One open only to him. He could hardly wait for the evening to arrive.

The fact that what he was contemplating held no time limit, no rules or restrictions as to when and where this particular game could be played, was beside the point. The success of the performance lay in the ritual. His entire life until this point rested on order and a sense of logical calm. Only thus had he been able to explore imaginative avenues in his mind, creating mental chaos out of that which had first to be arranged with the utmost consistency. Had this not been so, had he instead chosen to live in utter turbulence and random theorizing, grasping at philosophical straws – then he should have felt obliged to devote his whole life in another sphere. To that of returning all back to square one. Restraining those impulses in himself toward revolutionary logic, all that he held most dear. His entire existence was aimed naturally towards reversal. Towards questioning the established order of things. But that meant *there had to be an established order to question.* The same applied to his sex life. He had never before in his (almost) forty years of life ever donned the intimate apparel of a female. Except once, when forced to borrow a cousin's warm vest when his own had blown off the washing line and lain all morning in the snow. Oh, and another time at school when he had played 'the vicar's sister' in a Christmas production of *The Black Sheep Of The Family*, by L. du Garde Peach. Then, it was perfectly true, he had worn a pair of passion-killer bloomers belonging to the late and lamented wife of the Latin teacher. The entire lady's wardrobe had been awarded to Drama Props on her death.

But these occasions could hardly be said to count beside what he had in mind now.

He took a deep draught from his drink, swallowing it in one gulp. It was not his custom to drink on his own, but then the need to do so rarely arose. Blossom was always here. But even tonight, various invitations had arrived since Blossom's departure, he had turned down the offer of dinner with friends, or the chance of a couple of beers in the Boozer's Gloom and an impromptu meal with Gascoigne Teate, the landlord. But this evening he felt he needed to drink alone. It was his intention to become rather delightfully tight – after all, this could be seen as a celebration. The celebration of a new departure.

The garment Randolph chose eventually to wear was less figure hugging than this morning's, and altogether more alluring – possibly because of this. But he had chosen it for another reason besides the fit. He wished to conduct an experiment with himself. The outfit was the slinky black satin nightdress, side-slit to the waist, with the matching negligée edged with the froth of maribou feathers. This was the seductive set of garments which Blossom had been wearing on their last evening together in this room. The night that she had been swilling champagne and scoffing soft-centres. He had good reason to remember the climax – he didn't think he would be able to face another chocolate for the rest of his life.

He shut his eyes tightly and began his experiment, conjuring up the image of Blossom as she had been that night. She had been lying, one thigh exposed, on the floor at his feet. On this very spot which he occupied now.

He crossed his legs, just as she had, and the action caused the satin to slither further apart at the slit. He explored the opening with tentative fingers remembering the softness of his wife's limb, immediately below the profusion of pubic hair. He glanced down, then he frowned. Something was glaringly out of place – it was the lolling mound on his lap. His penis and testicles were giving offence, the sheer bulk of them brutalised the smooth surface of the satin nightdress. They should be tucked out of sight. Having crossed his legs, he now opened them, allowing his set to sink toward the floor. Then he pressed his thighs as closely together as comfort would allow. So far so good, now he had nothing – not even a crack! The folds of the nightdress flowed undisturbed from his hairy nipples, over his rib-cage, his abdomen, right down to the line of his thighs, and thence to his knees. Perfection. He closed his eyes again and this time with the memory of Blossom firmly in his mind he slowly began to caress himself.

And so it was and had been until the day of Blossom's return. The evening before had passed in the solemn ritual of parading slowly once (sometimes twice when the spirit moved him) around the bedroom, before the full-length mirrors. Each time he was adorned in an item of Blossom's vast collection of lingerie. And he wore a long ash-blonde wig, which he had discovered on her hat shelf, in addition to the discreet application of lipstick, rouge and eye-shadow. He had also discovered that wearing her perfume helped.

This interested him particularly, the sensory factor, and led directly to a regrouping of sub-sections in his notes. The last evening was the strangest of all, overhung with an aura of sadness, as he also recorded. It marked the conclusion of a fantasy. He very much doubted if such a period of time would occur again in his entire lifetime. The experience had been invaluable. The research had only just begun – for what he was starting to suspect would be his most important work. *The Spiritual Sperm* – A Proper Study of Spunk. The title had materialised during one climactic bout in a particularly pretty taffetta petticoat of Blossom's. No other title had ever come to him so easily.

Despite his secret idyll he could barely wait for Blossom's return. Although they had spoken each morning on the phone, he had been dreadfully conscious of the distance between them. Not just the physical distance – there was something else. There was a sort of hesitancy, a shyness. Or had that been his imagination? Possibly so. And of course the poor girl had the most fearful cold, one that would have made anybody sound quite unlike themselves. Hard luck that, going all the way to London and having to spend so much of the time in bed. Poor Blossom.

Poor Blossom was being mobbed by a long bus-queue of schoolboys who had spotted her alighting from the Daimler of the Director General of Universal Television. The Director General had just proposed marriage in the back of the car in the full hearing of the chauffeur. Blossom considered this to be in rather dubious taste, especially since the Director General was already married.

'You're married already.' She had voiced her objections in a cold severe voice.

'I'm married to a bottle,' he had answered balefully. 'And have been for the last fifteen years, for what it's worth.'

Blossom, moved to pity, had taken his hand in hers and squeezed it sympathetically. There was something very cuddly about this large, lonely man. In the past four months, since the switch-around, she had to admit she had really grown to be rather fond of him. But this was true of all the rest of June's men. She couldn't think what could have allowed June to leave them all for Randolph. No – that wasn't true! She could of course, because Randolph was and always would be the most marvellous man in the whole bloody world! Putting it another way , only the lure of Randolph could have influenced June into relinquishing the fame, the financial benefits, the freedom and the love affairs of her fabulous London life. Each morning that Blossom awoke (wherever it was, regardless of whose bed) she had to pinch herself to see if it was all really still true. But what fears she had had at the start!

It was difficult now to remember exactly whose idea the life-swap had been. Though circumstances had dictated subsequent events. From the moment of her, Blossom's, arrival in town, she had been mistaken for June. But the real crunch, the first turning point, they agreed between them – was when Randolph had mistaken June for Blossom on the telephone. And thank Christ that he had!

As it happened Blossom had missed Randolph's morning call by no more nor less than a mere fifteen minutes. A sixth sense had warned her that he might ring. Right in the middle of a passage of fine careless rapture with Professor Hamilton Hamilton, as he was moaning, 'June, dearest June – our very souls are in tune –,' and nibbling most effectively on the nub of her clitty, she just knew that at that precise moment back in Puddlemouth her husband was planning to speak to her. And she had rotated her pelvis at such alarming speed in her sudden agitation that she had almost torn the startled Professor's tongue from his throat.

'I'm coming!' she had cried out.

Then moments later, 'I'm going!'

And go she had, without so much as an explanation. Haunted all the way back to Flowers Hotel by the hurt bewilderment in the eyes of the Professor. 'But darling June – have I offended you? Tell me –' he had beseeched. But what could she have said! She could certainly not have told him the truth – that she was not June, but Blossom. Blossom behaving badly, Blossom being unfaithful, Blossom on the point of being found out . . . Jesus wept!

Her stomach had churned at the thought of poor Randolph's anguish, at the sweet baby's pain. What a blow! Shitballs – what a cunt she'd turned out to be! She sprawled back in the corner of the taxi mouthing a vehement stream of self-abuse.

The worst part of it was that she felt no genuine remorse. Her anxiety was simply the fear of being found out.

She leaned forward, and on impulse tapped the dividing glass to the taxi-driver's compartment. 'Could you stop at the next phone box, please?' She had hit on the answer. *She* would telephone Randolph now, she would beat him to it. She would say that her first thoughts had been of him as soon as she had woken, that she felt she just wanted to hear his voice. She would say all the things which she knew he was preparing in his mind to say to her. She rang. The line was engaged.

'You've just missed Randolph. He phoned about fifteen minutes ago. He was appalled by your terrible cold and said to stay in bed for the rest of the day.' June smiled groggily. 'But he was most concerned, he'll be ringing tomorrow about the same time. You have two alternatives, either catch my cold and develop as croaky a voice as mine – or let me answer, as you, again tomorrow morning.' She gave Blossom a quizzical look. 'That might be best – now that you've had a taste of the alley-cat's life, there's no knowing what time you'll return . . .'

And so it was that each morning Randolph and June would conduct lengthy conversations of the most loving intimacy. It was a revelation to June, the warmth and the teasing wit, the closeness, the kindness, the erotic overtones, the small hints, the outright bawdiness, the sensual insinuations.

She had always, of course, been immensely attracted (as who wasn't?) to her brother-in-law. By the end of the first week she had fallen in love.

'I can't believe, Bloss, that Randolph won't know in bed.' June was getting cold feet.

'Fucking, you mean?' Blossom was trying to decide which of June's outfits she should wear on the television this evening. It was the continuation of a group discussion that had been started the previous night. An important event, that had been, marking as it did the very first *professional* reversal of the two girls. Blossom had emerged so far with creditable aplomb.

'Yes, fucking – he'll see the difference.'

'I very much doubt it, kid.' Blossom had turned to smile reassuringly. 'You see the whole success of our sex-life rests on the illusion that I am very many different people. It means that he is living out his fantasies, if you like. So that he wouldn't ever expect me to be the same from one fuck to the next. I do different things all the time – just to ring the changes. You'll soon get the hang of it. And if you don't, well Randolph will simply assume that your stupidity is just another pose.'

'Thanks.'

But that was, more or less, how it happened. Randolph was so ecstatic to have Blossom back again that he noticed no difference in her at all. She struck him as possibly somewhat subdued, but then she'd had a long journey. Also she had just recovered from the ill-effects of that flu-bug. 'You could do with a holiday.' He had hugged her close. 'Don't go away from me again,' he'd whispered in her neck. And they had drunk a bottle of champagne to celebrate her return – and then another. They missed the meal they had intended to have in the one decent restaurant Puddlemouth possessed, because by that time they were busy in bed. June simply presented herself as she was, overwhelmed by the trembling beginnings of love. For some reason Randolph was inexplicably moved by his wife's tenderness. So much so that at the point of the first orgasm he began to cry. They came to climax together, their faces wet with the saltiness of his tears.

Blossom managed finally to escape from the mobbing schoolboys. She was looking in on a discussion being held by The Coordination Committee in Defence of the 1967 Abortion Act, made up of sixteen organisations including the Family Planning Association, the National Council for Civil Liberties, The Abortion Law Reform Association and many members who planned to back up pro-abortion MPs and influence parliamentary opinion. Picket lines were under discussion. The meeting was being held in Mortimer Street. At the entrance to the building, a feminist group had posted various slogan posters on the wall, including the graffiti depicting the corner of a tiled public lavatory with the scrawled message: When God Created Man She Made A Mistake. It was one of Blossom's favourites.

It had been Hilda Vengeance's idea that Blossom should come along. Hilda was the official legal adviser to the group and had been since its inauguration. They were a set of admirable girls, but Blossom knew that already, she had met many of them whilst recording her recent Female Series. She wholeheartedly supported their work. Unfortunately she was not in the position to stay long today, she only hoped that her brief visit would not be construed as a sign of her lack of interest. She had no wish to antagonise anybody. But although she was as scrupulous with her time as it was humanly possible to be (after all there were only twenty-four hours in the day!) she found that she was becoming increasingly vulnerable to criticism from all sorts of unexpected quarters. Her daily mail, delivered to Television Tower and opened by her two secretaries, contained open abuse from such diverse groups as the Milliners' Guild for never wearing a hat, to the Preservation of Rural Accents for the impersonality of her vowels. Her clothes and the styling of her hair were deplored. Speculative articles appeared discussing the fact that she had never chosen to marry. Several of them contained rather touching quotes from Tiny about their years together. 'I loved the girl dearly – I never did understand what exactly went wrong. Of course June was always very ambitious.'

June had rung up after reading the first of them. 'Sod that,' she shouted furiously. 'Trust that little turd to get in on the act! I'm surprised that he hasn't tried to creep back into your – my – bed.'

Blossom had laughed. 'I've got news for you –'

'You mean he has! Well, I tell you something – I shan't forgive you if you do. I had enough of that bastard!'

Blossom had laughed again. 'I shouldn't worry about that – I wouldn't begin to know where to fit him in even if I wanted to. By the way, that Czech film chap is back in the big city, he keeps leaving messages. What do you think I should do?'

June had snorted and then said cryptically. 'Well, it depends when you're next in front of the camera. I shouldn't see him the night before – it's too much of a risk. The girls in Make-up do wonders with black eyes, but it's not worth it. Everyone gets to know inside an hour and then they go round pulling your leg about it for weeks. And it could leak out further now that you're more of a celebrity – you don't want all that sort of thing in the papers do you? Oh, talking of the papers, isn't Zachary Ram going a bit overboard? Last week *and* this he's made mention of you in *Views*. It is becoming terribly obvious, even Randy was saying so –'

It was perfectly true that Zachary Ram was in danger of placing himself in a position of professional ridicule over June Day. Twice already his editor had had to have a word over the abuse of his powerful position as a critic. 'This, Ram, is not the place for the display of your personal obsessions. Up to several months ago your column was a hard core of positive and thoughtful criticism. Now it has deteriorated into the bashful scribbling of a lovesick schoolboy. Will you kindly conduct your wanking in the privacy of where the hell you care to. I positively refuse to carry it any longer on my pages!'

Zachary Ram had huffily offered his resignation, which his editor had grimly (and wisely) refused. Ram's column was widely read, his was a respected name amongst the readers of *Views*. Indeed, his name had already pulled a new and younger readership that the magazine had not enjoyed before Ram had started to write for them. This obsession with June Day was to be treated as a joke. It was a passing thing – for God's sake, everybody was obsessed with her at the minute. It was getting impossible to even pick up a newspaper or magazine without reading her name or seeing her photograph. Admittedly she had done a first rate job with those series of hers. She had lifted them out of the run of those rather pedestrian programmes by the very quality of her presence, the unaffected freshness of her forthright approach. She was that rare thing – an absolute television natural. There was an incandescence about her which glowed . . . The editor of *Views* abruptly checked his fey meanderings – he had begun to sound exactly like the more juvenile of Ram's reviews.

It was truly amazing how Blossom had taken to the medium of television. The very first time, of the group discussion, had not been the worst. She had sailed through that one, and the follow-up. But then she had not been on the screen by herself or with just one other person. She had been carried by the rest of the panel. She had also taken June's professional advice – two stiff gins drunk within fifteen minutes of appearing. Such that the spirit hits the stomach and begins to take effect just as you are needing the lift. It worked a treat. June had made her up a draught to drink from a flask. 'You down that in the lavvy so that no one can see. Otherwise you get the reputation of being a boozer. You get hospitality, but you can't rely on it. Some stations only give you a drink when it's all over – in case anyone goes over the top. And this is a live show – you're transmitting direct, so you may find it's like that. Best to take the flask just in case. You are sure now that you want to go through with it? Because I don't mind missing this one – they know that I have been confined to bed these last few days . . .'

But Blossom had been adamant. 'This may be my only chance to try it and as you say it's not important, even if I don't say a single word. Though I should be able to do that – after all the subject is something that I know enough about. Woman's

Changing Role in the Home. I probably have more than you to say on that.' And she had. In fact what Blossom had said on each of those evenings had in their way helped to establish June Day's reputation on television as being a fresh and original personality. One who, although being around for the last several years, was at last coming into her own.

'What is your opinion on that, Ms Day?' the chairman had addressed Blossom. The studio audience had waited expectantly for this attractive girl's reply.

'Sorry – how awful, I have just lost track of things. We were talking about wives and I was trying to remember the maxim. Would you like to hear it?' Blossom had smiled ingenuously.

The chairman and the rest of the panel made murmuring noises of assent. The discussion had reached a rather low point, it could do with a lift.

'Well,' Blossom had cleared her throat. 'I think this is it – I should know the saying well enough. My married sister has it pinned up –' June watching in, back at Flowers rose from her pillow as if in silent protest, praying that Blossom wasn't going to say what she thought she would. Down in Puddlemouth, Randolph, attired in a pair of peaches-and-cream satin cami-knicks seated before the very slogan to which his sister-in-law would refer, raised his glass toward the television screen. It was as if he were toasting his wife. The resemblance was uncanny this evening.

'A wife . . .' Blossom cleared her throat.

A person coughed in the audience. Everyone was waiting for the precious gem. All those present in the studio, the director in the control room, the technicians on the floor, the vision-mixers, the sound controllers, the programme researchers, the publicity people, the receptionist in the foyer to Television Tower, plus the car-park attendant who had popped in from the cold. Along with the waiting taxi-drivers, ordered to drive the participants of the programme home later. Not to mention the four million viewers watching in their homes (including the emotional Randolph and apprehensive June).

Blossom began again, suddenly aware of being the undisputed centre of attention and squeezing the last ounce out of it. Her eyes twinkled roguishly. Here it came at last. 'A wife is an appliance you screw on the bed to get the housework done!'

And the following evening. 'A wife is a poorly paid prostitute with only one client!'

The telephone switchboard was jammed each time.

The effect on Cherie Pye's negotiating power, over the fees which she was now in a position to demand on June Day's behalf, was instantaneous.

'My angel — you 'ave pushed your earning up by almost a 'alf! Is true! I know, I can 'ardly believe it myself. The telephone it is ringing so much for your services. You are making yourself free I 'ope during these next few weeks, *non?* This is important, very — to strike while the h'iron is 'ot!'

Blossom hadn't said a word. She had just answered the telephone call from June's agent. Afterwards she said to June, 'Christ, that woman sounds absolutely *ghastly*! I'm not sure, if we do the switch, whether I'm going to be able to stand her. That high-pitched squeal — it's just like a stuck pig, surely it must put people off dreadfully.'

June had shaken her head. 'You would think so, but it doesn't. She's a bloody marvellous agent. I don't think you would find a better one, but of course it's up to you. That's if,' she had added hastily, 'we decide to do the swap.' Though really they had each made up their mind by then.

There had been one or two moments of heart-pounding panic the following week when Blossom had been asked to do an interview, lasting less than five minutes (and thus needing to be concise) with a much heralded novelist from North Cornwall. This was a woman who had once been on intimate terms with Emily Shawl. Someone whom Emily had actually brought round to visit Blossom and Randolph several years ago in Puddlemouth.

Coming face-to-face with each other for the first time in the hospitality lounge, being briefed by the director as to the line of questions he would like to see pursued, the novelist refused to believe that she and Blossom had not met before. Despite Blossom's lengthy explanations that it would have been her twin sister and not her, the novelist remained unconvinced, as well she might. When the programme was suddenly on the air (a terrifying few seconds of countdown involving a beastly little light and someone waving their arms. And Blossom's throat as dry as the wings of a moth), Blossom completely forgot her briefed line of questioning. All she could think of was Emily Shawl's cruel comments regarding the famous novelist's inability to give a 'good gobbing'. Those had been Emily's wicked words. 'A good gobbing.' And those were the only ones uppermost in Blossom's petrified mind, until the woman herself took the bull by the conversational horns (aware that precious viewing time was being wasted and that she was there with the express intent of plugging her latest book).

Afterwards June sympathised. 'You "dried" there for a second, didn't you – isn't it awful! I've done that –' And she had gone on to tell Blossom that people did it all the time. Even old hands like nice Nobs Plater. He had done it the other day in the middle of reading the Ten o'clock News. Afterwards he had explained that it had been one of his chest pains again. Though it had been pointed out to him – he *had* eaten that evening in the studio canteen. He should expect to suffer the ill effects of indigestion after that. And he had been forced to agree that a man in his position with the nation's news at the tip of his tongue ought to be more careful what he put in his mouth . . .

But from then on Blossom's self confidence slowly grew. Since she could never be certain which people her sister was familiar with, she went around with a permanent half-smile on her lips. Colleagues began remarking to each other what an absolute pleasure she had become to work with, eager to listen, eager to learn their opinions, never tiring of the old clichés everyone trotted out in the pub, in the bar, in the studio canteen, on location. It was almost as if she had never heard any of it before. Suddenly she was everyone's favourite, with producers and directors clamouring to work with her. Success breeding success.

And so it was with her love-life. Blossom was positively bombarded with invitations to dinners, to film openings, to previews, to first nights. Dimples (who was now manageress of Flowers – Mercedes having returned to the States to star off-Broadway) said she had never known anything like it. Nor had Blossom. But there was no room for any further lovers in her life than she managed to fit in already. And she had no interest in straying from the small but passionate posse that June had bequeathed her. They were a diverse enough group to satisfy her demands – she was able to play a different role with each of them (which gave her the warm feeling that she was still in a way with lovely Randolph). And besides that, she felt a sense of responsibility toward them, just as June was taking care of

Randolph for her – so she, Blossom, must keep her sister's men under her wing.

She found that she had no favourites, though after, immediately after, being with each of them she would think that really *he* was the one.

Today she had lunched with the Director General after sucking him off in the grandiose seclusion of his office (an uneasy aperitif) with the distraction of secretarial sounds on the other side of the door – preferable to it being the other way around. The great man himself could have been caught by a member of staff tucking into what could have appeared to be a particularly scrumptious strawberry sandwich. For Blossom had her periods, a fact which never failed to excite the Director General. He seemed to revel in the gore. And although it made no difference at all to her sex-life with Randolph (they fucked throughout that time as if all was normal), she had never experienced the positive appetite for it that the Director General displayed. She sometimes wondered whether that hadn't been the basic reason behind his professional success – the fact that he was out for everyone's blood!

Today for instance he had greeted her at his desk (after she had been shown through the door by an overtly discreet secretary) with a white linen napkin tied ostentatiously around his jutting chin!

'Are we eating here?' She had glanced around the large room for signs of a cold buffet and champagne on ice. That, after all, had been the manner of their second luncheon together in this room. But no, there appeared to be nothing of that kind this morning.

And then she had got the message.

'Don't be a naughty boy!' she had scolded. 'No, I mean it. Take off that silly napkin – cunnilingus today is absolutely out of the question in my condition. No. Don't look like that. Really, whatever next! Your secretary would think you had a secret supply of raw steaks or were involved in some sacrificial rites on the sly – all that blood on your bib! Come on now, don't cry. I'll give you a nice cosy blow-job, really you're worse than a child!'

But they had a very relaxed lunch afterwards. He had taken her to The White Elephant in Curzon Street, which made sure that everyone in television knew. They would

115

immediately jump to the conclusion that this was a business luncheon, instead of what it was – the open evidence that they were having an affair. Cynthia, the Director General's wife, was possessed of a highly unpredictable nature. He could never be quite certain how she might react to any given situation. 'Alcoholics are so damned unreliable,' he would confide to Blossom, shaking his large head. His conversation was peppered with these kind of dull truisms. Blossom couldn't for the life of her understand how in hell he had managed to get a Double First, but then, as she'd keep reminding herself, she was used to the wit and wisdom of Randolph. And Randolph, when he was on form, could make Bertrand Russell look like Mickey Mouse. More or less.

Even so the Director General aroused what she supposed must be her maternal instinct, she cared a great deal about making him feel wanted. She felt that he had suffered short supply of love and sex during his life. Unlike Professor Hamilton Hamilton.

Professor Hamilton Hamilton had become obsessed with Blossom (believing her to be June) and June (believing her to be Blossom) as a twosome, with himself participating as the third in a sexual triangle. The idea had sprung to his mind during that very first dinner at The Gay Hussar when Blossom had masqueraded as June. It was because he knew that Blossom was in town (though as he had already been given to understand, she was confined to her bed with a beastly cold).

But he was impatient for her recovery, he could hardly wait to renew her acquaintance, as he kept telling his dinner companion.

'Tell me, June,' he had interrupted her in mid-sentence, 'had you and your twin-sister any desire for each other as small children. I mean did you explore each other's little bodies, that sort of thing?' Blossom had been surprised by the abruptness of the question. It was perfectly true that earlier they had been discussing the modern relevance of De Sade, over Victor's delicious Pike Quenelles. She gave proper consideration to the question. It was not the first time that it had been put to her, or to June for that matter. Many men appeared to find the possibility, that they would have discovered their sexuality together, immensely intriguing. Randolph had explored the subject often enough in the past. Though not for a

116

long time – she wondered about that. Perhaps because June had not visited for some while.

She had answered with an honesty that had completely disarmed the Professor. 'I think we were more aware of each other's bodies when we reached the age of puberty. We would certainly compare our pubic hair, such as it was. And our breasts of course, there was never, ever any self-consciousness. As to whether we masturbated together, well yes, I remember that we did. It was rather like when we were small babies. They used to find us asleep, each with a thumb in the other one's mouth. In the same way I would play with – (she had nearly tripped up then and said June!) Blossom. You know, rub her clitoris. And she would rub mine. It only felt as if I was playing with myself in a way. I always felt it would have been more fun if there had been a second person present. Not a *third* person – do you see what I mean? For example, just a little thing, but at precisely the same moment without either of us saying anything, we would both reach to our mouths in the middle of this mutual masturbation to transfer some lubricating spittle to our slits. And what's more we always, always came together, rubbing like mad. That was very exciting now I remember it. We were as sensitive with each other, knowing exactly where and how to touch, as we were with ourselves. It was self-masturbation really. And another thing, we were always horny, in the mood for that sort of thing at the same time. It was never a case of one of us not feeling like it, when the other did. But then when I (Christ! She had done it again – she *must, must* be more careful!), when Bloss and I went our separate ways – you know she got married to Randolph when she was only eighteen, then I suppose our sexual centres and horizons had altered. We have never caressed each other since then.'

'What a pity!' Those were the only words that the Professor had uttered. But he had seemed decidedly disturbed by what Blossom had confided. And there was a blazing light, which could be described as fanatical, shining behind his blue eyes.

Valentine, the fey and beautiful aristocrat, was quite a different kettle of fish. Describing her reaction to him, Blossom had admitted that half the attraction was that it made her feel as though she were actually fucking her own son. Fucking Pip – the erotic attractions of incest!

June had sniffed. 'Well, not having a son I wouldn't know

117

about that!'

'No but June, his body – he's so delicately made – didn't you find that. Like holding a child – no?'

'Not where it matters.' June had been rather churlish altogether about Valentine. She didn't really know why on earth she should have felt like that either. It certainly wasn't that she minded about sharing him – neither she nor Blossom harboured any corrosive jealousy over any of June's lovers, or Blossom's husband. It certainly would have meant the end of the life-swap if either of them had.

'Perhaps it's the druggy thing that I've taken against, Bloss,' June had tried hard to rationalize her disquiet. They had to be completely honest with each other over any doubts. 'I always felt so guilty, we just used to lie around rolling joints all day. I confessed as much, I had to, to Cherie one evening after I had split up with Valentine. And she nearly went berserk as you can imagine. All those times when she'd been trying to get hold of me for jobs. It would be a terrible waste for us, or rather you, to have got this far in your career just to have it go up in smoke.'

Blossom was aghast. And then she laughed. 'When did you last see Valentine?' she demanded.

'It seems like years, but of course it isn't. It's just that he's never given up hope, I suppose. I dread to think what he's like now though. I heard that he was on to speed, coke and heroin too. What do you think – has he gone completely to the dogs?'

But all Blossom would do was laugh again into the telephone. This was one of their daily conversations (from Blossom's private line at Television Tower, so that poor Randolph shouldn't be landed with the gigantic telephone bill at the end of the quarter). 'Perhaps I shall refuse to answer that one. I'll just keep you in suspense – better than that I might pop down one weekend and bring Valentine with me – what about that! For that matter – what about bringing them *all*? Say for Christmas!'

At that point Blossom had really meant it as a joke. At that point she had not yet spent time with the Czech film director. Nor had she seduced the hysterical Zachary Ram.

By Christmas she had done.

CHAPTER FOUR

Blossom Tree (really Blossom) lay in her own four-poster bed with her husband's body in her arms. They had enjoyed the very first fuck of the New Year. In a matter of hours she would be gone, to be replaced by June her identical twin.

Randolph Tree was fast asleep, the entire night (and the previous week) had been one of spent passion. With an exotic atmosphere of brooding lust hanging heavily in the air which he had been at a loss to explain. Though the easy explanation was there for all to see. His sister-in-law, June (really Blossom) had arrived for Christmas with the dazzling charisma of her current fame as the Television Celebrity of the Year. Or whatever she was now – perhaps it was Top Female Personality in the *TV Times* Readers' Poll. Blossom had explained it all, but he had been forced to admit to June herself that he had not taken as much account as had been expected of him. The reason being that these days his whole attention was on *Spunk* (his new book). She had laughed understandingly and listened with absolutely undivided concentration to the outline of the work, even questioning closely some of his tentative theories and offering a few suggestions of her own. What a good-natured creature this charming woman was! It never failed to please him whenever he was reunited with his wife's twin, to think that there were two such absolutely splendid girls in the world. Meaning (though God damn the ghastly thought) that if something ever happened to the one he was married to ... Along with her incredibly potent presence, which seemed to ignite the atmosphere, had arrived the most amazing assortment of men. They had come out of nowhere! Pouring into the house, every shape and every size! Or so it had seemed to the bemused Randolph.

'Who the hell are these people?' He had cornered Blossom (really June) in the kitchen.

'All my sister's lovers, I presume . . .' She had answered with what he considered to be an astounding calm, almost as if she had intimate knowledge of every sodding one of them. Though, when he came to think about it, she must have met some of them when she had gone up for her holiday in London. He was on familiar terms with Professor Hamilton Hamilton, though it had to be said that the change in the poor fellow had been rather shattering. From having been a person of considerable charm and essential dignity, certainly with the clear evidence of a first class mind, he now struck Randolph as being simply a benign old fool. Almost gaga. Of course June was to blame. He clearly adored her, otherwise why in heaven's name should he make such a fool of himself careering all over the countryside in pursuit of his idol. Oh yes, he'd got the hots for her alright – it was rather pathetic to witness. Him in competiton with so many men that much his junior.

Not that it was at all clear to an onlooker which of the assorted crew stood the best chance with June. For sheer physical beauty (though of too feminine an appeal for Randolph) he would have lain odds on the young Lord Valentine. The Czech film director certainly exuded a powerful brute force, there was no overlooking him. Him or his snarl! Nor was there any overlooking the chap who had the terrifyingly drunken wife in tow – the six-foot-four Director General. June had introduced him all around as her boss, but you didn't have to be a genius to see that there was more to it than that. The same with the clever little sod Zachary Ram. Randolph had enjoyed meeting him, he had been able to congratulate him on the bloody good job the chap was making of his Sunday television column. *The News* had made a shrewd move luring him away from *Views*. He was too bright to moulder away writing solely for a minority readership. That's what Randolph had been able to tell him.

But it had to be handed to June – she certainly kept her entourage under control! There was nobody flying at the others' throats. No scenes, no unpleasantness. Randolph could only wonder what sort of fools they were to be able to tolerate the situation. He certainly wouldn't have wished to share his wife in such a way!

Yes, it had been a strange week. Not as problematical as Blossom (still playing June) had expected. Christmas had passed in comparative calm. And there had been two of them to share the sexual load. She had doubts as to whether she would have been able to cope on her own!

It was with this solution in mind that she had purchased several suitably festive outfits in duplicate before leaving London. It was years and years since she and June had dressed identically, it might be fun (and clever) to do so this Christmas. June had agreed. To be perfectly honest, both girls were rather excited at the prospect of Christmas – June was very much looking forward to seeing the 'team' again. It had been her suggestion – that Blossom might care to sleep with Randolph for old times' sake. It was the least she could do in return for all the excitement that Blossom would be bringing with her.

Not that Blossom had expected the *whole bloody lot* to come!

It was amazing how many coincidences had suddenly materialised when each of them had learned that Blossom would be spending Christmas this year down with her twin sister in Cornwall.

'Puddlemouth,' Valentine had mused. 'Terrific surfing beach – yes, that's the place. Might be the very spot along that coast for the summer club I've been planning. A summer surfing club – a residential hotel on the beach, that would be the thing. "Valentine's by the Sea". What do you think? Christmas could be an ideal time to scout around for the right site . . .'

'Puddlemouth, not Puddlemouth in Cornwall? Good God!' Zachary Ram's vocal chords had careered off into the higher registers, as they did whenever he grew over-excited. 'My sister has just moved in that direction, near Lands End. She's gone to live with a potter. He's married. His wife continues to live on there as well, so I believe. It sounds a pretty cock-eyed set up, the sort of thing my sister would go for. She's trying to get me to go down there for Christmas. I had said no – but if you're going to be in the area . . .'

'Puddlemouth! Ha – what an extraordinary thing! A previous colleague and great friend of mine, now chairman of West Country Television, has a rather magnificent residence bang in the middle of Bodmin Moor. His wife went to school with mine, you know. And our children rather grew up with theirs – this was long before the old girl hit the bottle, of course. But I remember Puddlemouth quite well – don't they have that Arts Society there? Funny thing we were only discussing what to do

121

about Christmas the other day. Basil was ringing from Bodmin, bemoaning the sad fact that now the children had flown the nest, Christmas wouldn't be what it once was. Matter of fact, he suggested then that the old girl and I should consider spending the festive season with them. Your being in the same neck of the woods puts a brighter complexion on things. I know the old girl would be pleased as punch to go. Basil's cellars have rather a splendid reputation – she could be sozzled on the very best stuff . . .'

The Czech film director, riding on the crest of commercial success from *The Wing of the Rat*, had at last decided to begin shooting *Flying Fish* – a tense horror tale charting the first threat to the final extinction of an entire fishing community from a vast shoal of mutant fish which develop feathers and finally desert the ocean to flock the skies as predatory freaks, half-sprat, half-seagull. The location researchers had reported that Cornwall was the ideal setting for the saga. Hearing this the Czech director gave instructions that the tiny resort of Puddlemouth should be investigated since he himself had sound knowledge of a small fishing harbour there. A close friend of his would be spending Christmas in this place. It would be extremely pleasant if he could combine business with pleasure . . .

Professor Hamilton Hamilton had been the very first of the admirers to jump openly at the chance to be around at Christmas. He would really enjoy the opportunity to talk to Randolph once again. It was several years since they had been given the occasion for a lengthy discussion. He wanted to hear all about the extraordinary work that he had been given to understand Randolph was involved in at the minute. Was it really outright pornography? And he would be able to meet up with Blossom again. He had still not recovered from the disappointment of not getting together with her when she had been up in the summer. Now, at last, he would be in the company of the two girls together. He could barely conceal his impatience . . .

The girls had conducted many discussions over the phone regarding the arrangements.

'I think it has to be the rule, don't you, that no one can actually stay in the house – I mean we're not offering them a bed of their own.' June, who was in charge of the domestic arrangements (as mistress of the house) was anxious to know all these details.

Blossom agreed. 'Absolutely *not*. If you offered them a bed they wouldn't stay in it anyway. No, that's understood. Anyway, let's go through the list. The Director General will have what's her name – "four sheets to the wind" – in tow anyway. I should expect him over here about once, wouldn't you? And we three, you and Randy and me, will be invited over to Bodmin for dinner. We'll probably go, could be fun seeing how the other half lives.'

'What about Zachary Ram?' June still couldn't come to terms with the thought of Zachary Ram as one of the team. Well, that wasn't so strange because, as Blossom pointed out, he was the only one that June hadn't screwed yet. Though according to Blossom, he was quite an impressive performer, with great stamina and the biggest cock of the lot.

'Zachary? Oh well, he'll be staying with his sister, though of all of them I should think he'll be the one to try and wangle something. Because he's already explained to me that whatever he does he has to be near a television set over Christmas Day and Boxing Day – he has to file his copy for the following Sunday. Well, if he is over here, what will he do? Will we expect him to drive, pissed, back to Lands End? It seems a bit anti-social.'

They both thought about it. Blossom came up with the answer. 'If he expects to come over for both days, we should book him into Emily Shawl's for the night –'

June nodded, but dubiously. 'Perhaps we should stagger it a little. Perhaps coming over for both days is one day too many. Let's decide who'll come on each of those days. Nobody should come for both. I think Zachary Ram should have Christmas Day with his sister and come over here the day after. We know the Director General and Pissypops will be with their pals. We shall see either before, or after, the two crucial days.'

'Which leaves us with Professor Hamilton Hamilton, Valentine and –'

'And the European sadist! Will the Czech be arriving with members of his crew – surely not over Christmas?' June was surprised what a flickering anticipation she harboured at the thought of his arrival. *The Wing of the Rat* had been showing locally much to the fury of Pip and Willow who had not managed to con the desk that either of them was over eighteen. But she and Randolph had been to see the film and had enjoyed it immensely.

'He is one of June's, the director.' June had been able to say when the name had come up on the titles.

'Good chap, I'm sure,' had been Randolph's rather abstracted reply. He had been pondering the application of a violent stimulation technique employed by the early Etruscans, as a means of maintaining an amazing extension of the male orgasm, without shrivelling the scrotum in the process. The shuddering foetus of an animal, ripped from the womb and used as a gripping background to the titles of this film, had reminded him somewhat of his own research. This Czech director must be a bit of a pervert, getting his rocks off on this sort of stuff.

'Is he a bit of a pervert? Does June say?' He asked June at the end.

'Why do you ask?' she asked innocently. The depravity of the film's violence had excited her. She even found that she was now squeezing Randolph's fingers rather more tightly than necessary as they strolled home through the darkened streets. Not because she was nervous, but because it gave her a small thrill to think that she might be hurting him.

'Ouch!' he exclaimed, suddenly conscious of the spiteful pressure, then adding rather irritably, 'Go easy on those fingers. I'll need them in the morning for typing, if you don't mind.'

June thought how much more pleasurable it would have been if he had landed her a blow round the chops.

'Ah – the European sadist!' Blossom had laughed softly, thinking with great affection of the violent bouts she had enjoyed with this tame brute. June had exaggerated the dangers. Why, these days Blossom had no fears at all of black eyes or similar trophies. Not on *her* body at any rate, though she felt proud of the liverish bruise *he* still bore to the left of his jaw. Not to mention the neat bite from the lobe of *his* ear. She still recalled the actual sensation as her front upper teeth met her lower – that, and his animal bellow of pain. Good fun.

'Well, the sadist is bringing his writer with him, and several others I believe. They don't celebrate the birth of our Lord you know – it's against their political beliefs. They're no more believers than we are, so there isn't any reason why they shouldn't be working all through Christmas.' Blossom spoke with what June considered to be an unnecessarily condescending tone.

'Fuck all that,' she said loudly. 'I'm not some sodding country bumpkin, I'm thinking of the Unions. He won't be coming with any of the crew members will he?'

Blossom chuckled down the phone. 'Keep your hair on – by the way I'm considering a change of hair colour again, are you?'

'Funny you should mention it – what about blonde?'

'Yes. I'd thought of blonde. Do you think my public would stand for it?'

June interrupted her, 'Never mind about that – do you think my husband will?'

Each laughed contentedly, then Blossom said suddenly, 'It will be funny I must say. Seeing him.'

'And seeing the children again,' June added. 'And me.'

They went together to have their hair bleached and restyled, emerging from the hairdresser's like two sophisticated schoolboys. Platinum blonde, as blonde as Jean Harlow or Mae West. But crew-cut.

'You don't think this is going too far, do you Mrs Tree?' the hairdresser said anxiously to June. 'It's not you that I'm worried about, it's your sister. After all she is a celebrity. And the public is a funny thing, it likes to know where it is – you know what I mean. It gets used to seeing someone the way they are and then resents any drastic change.'

'Oh, bugger all that!' Blossom exclaimed gaily. 'Let's take the whole bloody lot off, that's what I say!'

'Well, if you're sure, Miss Day,' the poor girl had answered, concealing her private reservations. She had always thought that Mrs Tree was a little bit eccentric, her twin was obviously just as bad.

The end result was amazing. The entire salon had crowded round the two blondes. One on her own would have looked extraordinary enough, but the two of them together was truly uncanny.

'This is our most stylish – wouldn't you say, June?' Blossom (the real Blossom) had let the name June slip out without thinking.

The hairdresser looked from one to the other. Surely it had been Miss Day that had been sitting on the right, hadn't it? And yet Mrs Tree was addressing her remark to the twin on the left. Or had they switched around when they had returned from the driers? That must have been it – for a moment there she had felt thoroughly confused. It didn't help matters that Mrs Tree was of a modern kind and so had never worn a wedding ring. That would have been one way of telling the two of them apart. Or if they were dressed differently. But no, identical from top to toe. Same jade green all-in-one sort of jumpsuits, latest London style (matching their eyes). Same honey-coloured cowboy boots (several shades deeper than their new hair). Only their coats were different, which was how the hairdresser had distinguished between the two as they had arrived for the appointment. Mrs Tree had been wearing her usual shaggy fur, racoon, that's what she called it. And there was no mistaking it. Once seen, never forgotten, like all of her clothes. Whereas Miss Day had come in wearing what looked like a very smart leather gentleman's overcoat, tightly belted with a huge stand-up collar. The same sort of honey colour as her boots. There was no doubt about it – they were an eye-catching pair. There were not many as eye-catching in Puddlemouth. Or anywhere come to that. There being two of them.

The twins looked at each other. Each knew what the other was thinking. The slip over the name had triggered off a new plan of action. Of course – why not revert back to being themselves! Just while Christmas lasted . . . They moved toward the door and took their coats from their hangers. June reached for the leather. Blossom wore the racoon, always her favourite winter coat. She had forgotten how very warm it was.

Professor Hamilton Hamilton maintained his erection throughout the Christmas dinner. He didn't want to, it was too damned uncomfortable for words. But there was simply nothing to be done that would ease the situation. Except the obvious of course.

And that for the time being was out of the question.

But he had plans.

The astounding (and immensely arousing) thing was that he simply could not tell the two girls apart. And though he had expected there to be this striking similarity, having never seen the two of them together like this, he had not imagined that it would have been this confusing.

Take this wonderful meal (wonderful though marred by the presence of a saturnine foreigner and a foppish English aristocrat) for instance. Each time either of the girls rose to bring various dishes to the table, and quite often they would be doing so together (each being as familiar with the kitchen as the other), he found that unless he actually kept his eyes on the one that he *knew* to be June then all was lost. He was completely at sea. There was absolutely no distinguishing between them. And what's more he couldn't even be sure that they were not playing a special sort of game between themselves. To deliberately confuse the guests still further.

More than once he had caught the dazzling clear green gaze of one of them settling on him with a special look of intimacy. This is June, he had been able to say to himself, reassured. Only to be the recipient of the same sort of meaningful half-smile from the other twin at the far side of the room. I was wrong, this must be June, he had been forced to correct himself. Which, he now wondered, had he made hurried love to this afternoon whilst helping with the washing-up. It had been a silent and short copulation, the most intense that he had experienced for some time. Schoolboy stuff, with the dreadful fear of imminent discovery – the rest of the household only up there around the bend of the stairs. All waiting to go for a wintry walk on the shore.

But he had to have her. There were no words spoken, not a single one.

She had been standing at the sink, preparing to tackle the saucepans. He had watched her tying a pinafore around her narrow waist, a striped red and white one. Curving over her flat belly and provocative hips, accentuating the tight fullness of the buttocks.

The atmosphere between them was tense with sexuality – he surely wasn't imagining that! If he was, she made no move to indicate that his attentions were in any way unwelcome. Though to suggest to him that time was of the essence, she had glanced warningly at the scarlet kitchen clock on the wall.

He understood this. With an economy of movement he had brought her hips to his, skilfully unzipping his flies whilst slipping down the elasticised waist of her soft woollen slacks and the underlying tights. Then he plunged his prick in.

She was facing away from him, still at the sink, with a Brillo pad in one rubber-gloved hand and a soup-stained saucepan in the other. As he reared and bucked behind her, his fingers pressed around her front, amongst her pubic hair, to make sure that his excited penis should explode in the right hole. She bent forward from the waist to make this doubly certain. Once or twice, in his extreme rapture, he had withdrawn too far and in struggling to get back in had knocked on the wrong door. Buggery was all very well, but not best done in such desperate conditions. Not poised over a bowl full of Fairy Liquid.

Then he had come, panting and clutching onto the strings of her pinafore. Grappling to re-adjust his clothing and hers as he heard voices drifting from the stairs. Hers first, since her hands were full – she had begun to scrub furiously with the Brillo around the inside of the saucepan leaving him to return her to respectability. He liked that. It showed trust. But the sacrifice caught him short, there was no time now to see to his own flies. People were here, they were pouring into the kitchen. Randolph was leading the way, followed closely by the young ones, Pip and Willow. Everyone seemed to be carrying a kite. The Professor felt faint, small specks of silver light suddenly appeared before his eyes. But he had the presence of mind to grab a dish-cloth from the draining-board and clutch it to his flagrant groin, fumbling beneath it to locate the lip of his zip. It had been a debilitating moment, quite ageing in a way, and it evidently showed on his face. Randolph had stepped back, staring. 'Professor – are you feeling yourself?'

Even that question had come as a shock since feeling himself was precisely what the Professor had been doing. His groping fingers beneath the dish-cloth had just come into contact with the slightly tacky surface of his still swollen cock. Nothing seemed to be in the right place.

He brought his hand guiltily to his face, leaving only one holding the fort. 'Feeling myself!' he echoed. His voice sounded hollow. The enchanting creature at the sink remained silent though her shoulders shook slightly. No one could see her face.

He dearly wanted to reassure himself that she was not in tears. The last thing in the world that he would have wished was to cause her distress. Now several of the others were staring at him too. The handsome effete young man, the cheerful son, and his sister. The sister was whispering, she was whispering to her father. At her words Randolph laughed out loud. 'Willow seems to think that you may need the lavatory and are much too polite to ask!'

'The Czech looks rather cheesed off – do you need any help?' Blossom was preparing to pour the brandy over the Christmas pudding, whilst June was busy with the white sauce.

June glanced over her shoulder towards the table. 'He shouldn't be. I gave him a bit in a gorse bush, his bum's scratched to smithereens. Didn't you notice? This afternoon we flew the kite to the top of the cliff. We were gone for about half an hour. I felt sure that you had noticed.' June looked at Blossom's face.

'Oh, I get it – you look like a cat who's been at the cream! Valentine?'

Blossom nodded. 'In your bedroom – we came back before the others. You remember, to put the kettle on for tea . . .'

It was necessary to keep checking with each other. As Blossom pointed out, they really ought to make a list as to who had had whom. Because if they were not careful, some greedy people would be getting more than their fair share. Doubling up, without them being any the wiser.

Randolph was the one who inadvertently found himself to be in that fortunate position. Like everyone else he had been bowled over by the new image that Blossom and June had presented. Though he had never said so he had always hankered after having a blonde in his bed. There was something so aesthetically pleasant about the sight of blonde hair on black satin sheets. And now that is what he had. And though loyalty to Blossom would have forbidden him from putting it into words, there was something decidedly erotic about having the two of them together in the house. Both blonde, both so exactly alike in their clothing. The whole set up delighted his senses. But he still prided himself on knowing which one was which – Christ he bloody well should after all these years!

On Christmas morning he arose at his usual time, it was still dark, the first light had yet to break. He yawned and stretched. Blossom lay sleeping soundly in their bed. He looked at her lovingly then bent to kiss her mouth. She was ravishing, she was wearing a pearly white cotton nightgown, one with long sleeves and a ruffle of lace around the neck. The sort worn in times past. This summer she had used it as a summer dress on the beach, slipping it over her bikini. He had remarked then how well it suited her. But now with her short blonde hair she looked like a choirboy, or a cherub. She stirred beneath his kiss, arching her torso unconsciously as she slept. Randolph observed the shape of her breasts reform under the loose folds of the nightgown, twin pinnacles of cotton catching on her nipples. It was warm in the bedroom, they had reset the central heating to counteract this cold spell. The top coverings of the bed had been thrust low enough for Randolph to glimpse the cleft of his wife's buttocks, in which the nightgown had somehow got awkwardly trapped. She had rolled over and now lay as if in the womb, one leg higher than the other. Vulnerable. He sat on the edge of the bed feasting his eyes. Should he take her now, or should he do the usual thing – let her sleep and then have a session at a more reasonable hour.

His cock was fully erect, he looked down at it affectionately. 'That's all right, you greedy little sod – let's get upstairs and do some work. Plenty of time later for what you have in mind.' It didn't occur to him to masturbate. Since Blossom's return in the summer he had not done so once. With her handy, wanking seemed a terrible waste.

But his decision, he regretfully had to admit, was not very conducive to concentration. His research was not aiding matters. Studying Lo Duca's profusely illustrated *A History of Eroticism*, he found his thoughts wandering. Titillated initially by *The Turkish Bath*, a painting of voluptuous nudes by Ingres; he then found himself staring fixedly at the censor-cut shots of Brigitte Bardot's bare arse and suspenders from her film *Love is My Profession*. The shot is of her perched, skirts hitched and no knicks, on the edge of her lawyer's desk. She is offering him payment in the flesh. Lucky devil. Randolph leafed over without reading, until he came to three small frames from a French 'stag' film of 1925 (from *Sittengeschichte des Gehtemen und Verboten*, Vienna,). Then he gave up his attempt to work as a bad job. After all it was bloody Christmas Day – he could surely afford to take one day off. His brain wouldn't atrophy in that time and he felt he deserved to have the morning in bed with his wife. He sensed a special loving in her these last few days. He couldn't put his finger on it but it had been ever since the arrival of June. But then he might be wrong, it could be that he was approaching her differently. As if estranged yet, at the same time, sexually excited by her new blondeness. It was almost as if he were fucking a different girl! He gazed out at the calm sea, curiously calm today – yesterday it had been wild and too dangerous to swim. They had been forced to content themselves with simply skipping around in the surf, occasionally risking a daring dive beneath a particularly spectacular wave for the sheer fun of it. But being careful that at no time should any of them get out of their depth. Only last week a stranger had fallen to his almost instant death on this small bay, and swept out to sea before the rescue boats could do anything. The currents were absolutely treacherous with these tides.

Time for coffee. He would go and make one for himself and take one up to Blossom, but before that just a last lingering look at the cold apricot sky and the flat shining expanse of water disappearing to the horizon. As usual the sight filled him with elation.

It was in this mood, a mixture of spiritual serenity and sexual anticipation, that he descended the stairs on his way to the kitchen. He paused for a second at the closed door to his bedroom, thinking to enter. The inviting image of Blossom's rump had intruded on his mind's eye, it would be interesting just to investigate whether or not she was still asleep. But he decided against it, he really felt the need for a cup of coffee – to give him a quick boost for what he had in mind.

But she had beaten him to it! She was down in the kitchen already preparing coffee for him. He could smell the aroma drifting up the stairs even before he had passed the half-landing leading to June's bedroom. Oh, the darling! He hurried down. No one else was up, the rest of the house wouldn't be awake for ages even though it was Christmas Day. He suspected that the kids would have opened their bedside presents last night, reasoning that by the time they had got to bed, well past midnight, it was already Christmas Day. There wouldn't be a sound from them for some time. Or June for that matter – not the way that she had rammed into the Remy Martin last night. She would have reason to regret that this morning! So, the way seemed to be clear. Blossom all to himself, a nice breakfast all on their own. But first . . .

'No Randy!'

'I insist.'

'But Randy –'

He had stripped her crimson kimono from her shoulders, finding to his pleasurable surprise that she had removed the demure and voluminous white cotton nightdress. This flimsy garment was altogether easier for the rape which he was perpetrating. Blossom enjoyed his rapes, they had discussed it in a detached fashion many times in recent months after he had violated her in this manner. But today her protesting struggles were really authentic. She knew how much her resistance excited him . . .

Rounding the stairs in her white cotton nightdress, yawning and rubbing her pleasurably prickly scalp (like a hedgehog, her short hair felt – or an unshaven cheek) Blossom paused on this Christmas morning. She thought she heard noises – were those kids up already!

She was coming down to check the turkey which had been in the oven all night on regulo 1, ensuring that it would be beautifully tender for this evening's dinner. It was also her intention to make coffee for herself and Randolph, he must surely be feeling like a cup by now. The question of whether June would appreciate being woken with the hangover she would be suffering this morning was something she hadn't yet decided.

She stood still, perfectly still. There was no doubt about it, there were people in the kitchen. There was a definite scuffling now and a suppressed snortling sound, accompanied by the unmistakeable heavy gasping of humans screwing . . .

'Fucking arseholes!!' Blossom caught her breath on her own involuntary expletive. It was just that the sight before her eyes was not what she had been expecting. Perfectly true she had anticipated a scene of vigorous fornication, with one of the participants being her sister. But she had not thought that her husband would be the other. It had crossed her mind that one of the team might have made it his business to arrive before the others — on the principle that the early worm catches the bird. But she was quite unprepared for it to have been Randolph.

She peered, fascinated, around the entrance into the kitchen. The sexual charade was being enacted beyond and through the open-plan dining area. Placed here at this hidden juncture, behind the giant dinner-gong, no one could witness her — observing.

It had often passed through her thoughts, the image of Randolph and June having it off. Many, many times since they had embarked on the life-swap she had tried to visualise it. Whereas at first she had preferred to blot it out of her mind, for fear of experiencing an oblique sensation of pain, she had later come mentally to face it more and more. She wasn't jealous, she had never ever been jealous of June, of her twin. She couldn't be that. Such an emotion would be like being in competition with herself. It wasn't possible, not to be in competition — yet at the same time it was on the cards to wish to improve. To improve on past performances, to excel, to do better. In the case of making love and giving pleasure to Randolph it had always been Blossom's obsession to provide him with the greatest possible erotic enjoyment. These last couple of days and nights she had been going easy, letting him lead the way, encouraging but never taking the initiative as she used to before June had assumed the role of wife. Because with June, Randolph had seemed to have taken a different sexual role. More imaginative, more mannish, more perverted (if that was the right word) than he had been when she (Blossom) had been the instigator of their sexual games. His entire life was bound up with the subject these days, and for many years to come (so he had assured her joyfully) with the work he was writing. *Spiritual Spermatozoa – Significant Spontaneity* – The new title, now changed from *Spunk*. (*Spunk* being confusing to the British possessor of the lending library card, as also meaning 'pluck').

A rather fearful gagging noise now engaged Blossom's rapt attention. She peeped, recklessly taking a further step into the kitchen. Despite herself she found the experience of watching this tremendously arousing. She couldn't remember having had the pleasures of voyeurism before, but the circumstances — the fact that it was her own husband and her double (herself

133

really) that she was privileged to watch, that made it even more arousing.

But what ferocity, what vigour, what brutishness he was displaying. This was rape! June was struggling, but to no end. Randolph's large hand was clamped over her mouth, from whence issued these strangulated guttural sounds. The poor girl appeared to be choking, but that made no difference to her fate. Her assailant was hell bent on getting his end away. Blossom's throat was dry with excitement. She thought of the time that she had ventured across the moors waiting to be picked up by Randolph in his big black limousine. That occasion had been one of pre-arranged rape. Since then she had not had the pleasure.

It only occurred to her now – Randolph must be under the impression that he was raping *her*! This was not a glimpse of clandestine infidelity at all! He had mistaken June for her – Blossom – the implications began to dawn on her. They had obviously not yet fully dawned on June (though she was to be forgiven for not thinking too clearly at this moment). She was struggling *too* much! June was playing it for real, anguished by the knowledge that Randolph was being unfaithful with her, the sister of his wife. Except that he wasn't – it couldn't be counted as that, not if he believed this person he was poking was his wife. *He must never, ever, be made aware that this was other than the truth*! Blossom felt this most strongly. If he knew of their life-swap, if he began to have any inkling that this was what the two of them had been up to, she knew the whole thing would crumble.

She couldn't have explained why, but in her mind it was extremely important to preserve the precious structure of her marriage. It seemed to her that the success of it rested on the foundation of absolute fidelity. She considered that she had continued to remain loyal and true to her husband. So far she had not once had intercourse with any other man throughout their entire marriage.

Not whilst she was being herself.

The affairs, the fucks, the sexual encounters, all the lovers since the life-swap had occurred whilst she was being June, not Blossom. The very first time with Professor Hamilton Hamilton, she had gone to bed with him as her sister – and he had never guessed that it had been otherwise.

She would have hated it to be common knowledge that Randolph Tree was a cuckold. He was too fine (he was too famous) a person to be tagged as that. And of course he could well, if he came to hear of any indiscretions on her part – he could very well start a little dallying of his own. What's sauce for the goose . . .

This way it was better, it was getting the best of both worlds.

She thought speedily about how to handle this current and potentially crucial situation.

June must be made aware that she, Blossom, was in the know. And that there was to be no spilling the beans to Randolph, above all. If she could catch June's demented attention over Randolph's heaving shoulder, she would give her the sign that everything was under control, that for the next hour or so she (Blossom) would pretend to be June. Would return to June's room and emerge at a time more convenient to all, giving June (and Randolph) a chance to collect themselves and present a proper public face. Then perhaps she (Blossom) would take over again . . .

Randolph was completely carried away on a dense wave of lust. He was having more than a little difficulty in breathing, his senses pounded. There was a dull ringing in each eardrum, accompanied by what sounded like a celestial choir. Christ Almighty, he had never heard music before! At one stage he had become dimly conscious that the struggling body beneath his own had suddenly slackened, passed through a brief period of limp inertia, and then had begun rocking in a thrilling rhythm tight with his own. He was aware that at the point of orgasm he shouted out. Afterwards he felt faintly bilious. And surprised to hear the strains of the heavenly choir still ringing in his ears.

The Salvation Army were singing carols in the street.

'That was a close shave – I djdn't think that I would ever get your attention. To tell you the truth I was thinking of banging the gong. Randy wouldn't have noticed, he was really far gone.' Blossom giggled with June. They were comparing notes, keeping each other right up to date. Though that close shave had taken place almost a week ago, it gave both of them great amusement to relive certain highspots of this memorable time.

Tomorrow was New Year's Eve, they were sitting in Blossom's bedroom putting the finishing touches to the costumes that they would be wearing at the Puddlemouth Society of Arts Fancy Dress Ball. They intended going as Tweedledum and Tweedledee. Of course.

The following morning Blossom would be leaving for London. It would be the first day of the New Year and in the evening she would be appearing on a new television quiz show as the mystery guest. From then on Cherie had booked her work through to the middle of the month. Personal appearances, radio programmes, magazine articles, photographic sessions. A gruelling few weeks, but it had reached the stage as Cherie had pointed out, where it was important to keep June Day's name in the public eye. Her career had to be carefully nurtured if it was to continue to be a success. They were already having difficulty in deciding whether or not to agree to a further Female Series. Cherie was tempted by the colossal fees that she had managed to negotiate. And yet she felt, as Blossom did, that there might be a definite sense of *déjà vu* in yet another series about women. Although this one would pursue the theme of women as entertainers, comic entertainers. Pure humour. And Blossom was very much drawn to the principle, especially since the plan would be to investigate countries other than Great Britain. She rather looked forward to a trip around the world. Even so she could not come to a decision. A sixth sense warned her to wait, she had the feeling that there was something bigger in the offing. So she and Cherie were holding fire, they had until the end of January to make up their minds. In the meantime, Cherie advised her to spread herself around the media as much as possible. She felt Blossom (believing her to be June) had been away long enough. It would be almost ten days since she had left London.

'Let's have a look at you then, you two!' Pip and Willow had barged into their mother's bedroom to inspect Tweedledum and Tweedledee. They were about to be collected by their friends to spend tonight and New Year's Eve, and the following day on the friends' farm in the wilds where they bred lots of ponies. It meant that they wouldn't be seeing their mother again to say goodbye, but they were not aware of this. They were coming to say farewell to their celebrated aunt, so they thought.

Blossom kissed them, and hugged them very hard. It still surprised her how easily she could leave them. There was no pain at the parting. She wondered how they would have reacted to the knowledge that it was their true mother who was choosing to leave them. Would they have cried then? And would she? But this way, thank Christ, there were no emotional scenes. She had made a special point of studying the two of them very carefully over Christmas. It had been an inspired notion that she and June should revert back to being themselves. It had given Blossom a better chance of judging the reactions of Pip and Willow to herself, as their real mother. Had she noted any alarming symptoms of neurosis she would have reconsidered continuing with the life-switch. So far she had seen nothing to disturb her. She was certain that June was as warm and reassuring a mother figure as herself. There were certainly no worries in that direction. As Randolph so often declared, all that children really require is one positive touchstone. They had enough to cover a pebble-beach. She watched them now, kissing June.

'Bye Mum.'

'Bye Mum, mmm, you smell delicious.'

'Goodbye, my darlings. Have a lovely time – see you don't fall off any bloody ponies! We don't want to start the New Year with any broken bones –'

'No bloody fear, Mum –'

Blossom went to the top of the stairs to listen to the fragments of their disappearing conversation.

'She means *you* when she says falling off.' Pip's voice floated up accusingly.

'*Me*! You spiteful sod! She means you, if she means any bugger!' Willow's indignant answer sounded faint.

Blossom had the motherly instinct to shout down. 'And who the hell is *she* – the cat's mother?' But she didn't.

CHAPTER FIVE

Nice Nobs Plater collapsed whilst reading the Ten o'clock News on New Year's Eve. As a chilly cynic remarked, it was the final news flash of the dying year and turned out to be Nobs Plater's last.

But Blossom had no knowledge of the tragedy, not until she had managed to get the morning newspapers at Plymouth, running like a mad thing from the London train. The sad news was splashed over every front page.

He had suffered a fatal coronary before the entire nation. Being the professional that he was (a newscaster for fifteen years) he had reached the end of the news before keeling over, clutching violently at his heart. The reports suggested that he had died on the spot. Reading of the event Blossom felt a genuine tear spring to her eyes. Everyone liked nice Nobs Plater, a simple and uncomplicated man. Superbly suited to the job in hand. Grave and serious when the news required him to be so. Jaunty, even faintly flirtatious, when the occasion warranted a spot of jollity. A decent fellow, an all round popular chap, with not an ounce of ill-will in his entire body. It was, according to almost all of the editorials, as if a national monument was no more. The banner headline on the newspaper with the widest mass circulation read: *Nightie, night – Nobs!*, and beneath it in smaller print: *Alas – no more tomorrows!* 'Nightie, night – see you tomorrow.' That was how he had always ended his news readings.

'Snuffed it, poor sod!' the chap at the station news-stand had quipped, seeing Blossom stare. She had nodded. There would have been no point in disagreeing. She thought about it all the way to Paddington, about the implications and the repercussions of so sudden a death. What had he, poor old Nobs, been planning to do after the news. How would he have decided to see in the New Year. Certainly not in the way that he had!

She tried to think what she and June had been up to at the exact time of his departure from life. Had they not been leaving somewhere – the cocktail party at Basil's on Bodmin Moor? Or was that earlier – yes it must have been, because they could not have got back in time to see the New Year in at the Art Gallery otherwise. Although Randolph had driven like a demon. He was actually far from being sober. It would have been safer for them all to have accepted the offered lift in the Director General's chauffeur-driven Daimler. Randolph had pig-headedly refused to do that, he didn't care to abandon his own car on Bodmin Moor. Blossom secretly crossed her fingers all the way. But June had been prevailed upon to travel with the Director General. The Society of Arts Fancy Dress Ball was where he wished to see in the New Year. The real reason was that he was determined not to let June out of his sight. He had not yet had the chance of a Christmas poke.

It wasn't for want of trying. More than once he had manoeuvred it so that he and June should slip away from the cocktail party for a little spot of how's your father. 'How's your father' was the term that his friend Basil had used with a rather coarse wink, when the Director General had confided in him yesterday. It wasn't an expression that he was overkeen on himself and, as he had tried explaining to pal Basil, what he felt for this girl just wasn't like that. He had fallen deeply in love with her – further than that, he wanted her to be his wife.

Basil hadn't been able to see it. 'I know how it is, old man, you don't have to tell me. We all get as much as we can on the side, who doesn't in this game. But as for any marrying malarky – I should forget about that. For one thing you wouldn't ever be able to get rid of the old girl, old Cynthia, not without it costing you a bomb. And why bother? She turns a blind eye to whatever you get up to doesn't she?'

'A boozy eye,' the Director General said glumly. He was not too happy with the direction that this conversation had taken. Of course Basil had always been a crude bastard. It had been a mistake to confide his finer feelings to such a fellow, it had cheapened the whole thing. He didn't like discussing June as if she were anybody's whore. She was just not that sort of a girl.

He had missed her like hell this last week, and though they

o

had spoken on the telephone as often as he had been able to escape from poor old Cynthia's drunkenly amorous clutches, it wasn't the same as seeing the wonderful child. And child was how he had come to regard her in the warmth of his growing love. As something golden and pure, as someone radiant and good who had come to him to bring life to his life. He wondered at these times of highly-charged emotional thoughts whether he might not be becoming a little senile. The first signs of an inner softening! For instance, in his daydreams, he and June were already married. More – she was carrying his child. She was pregnant with the son that he had never had. Her youthful body was bearing the fruit of their union. His entire existence seemed to have been geared to this fresh start. Cynthia was the only fly in the ointment.

It had been the hope of the Director General to have been able to slip off alone to the Fancy Dress Ball with June, he had already alerted his chauffeur that this would be his intention. But on returning from this mission to his despair he learned that Cynthia was aware of his plans. Not only was she coming too (she was upstairs at this very moment devising a fancy dress for herself and Basil's wife), but she had inveigled others of the party to come along too. There would be three car-loads in all.

But at least the Director General sat next to his love.

They had arrived in Puddlemouth by eleven-fifteen or so. All three cars stopping outside the Puddlemouth Society of Arts Gallery to disgorge the human content. The Director General noted to his annoyance that there had been enough room in the other two cars to have allowed him to travel on his own with June, had they managed to have given the extremely inebriated Cynthia the slip. His wife (how he winced at the term) had kept up a manic chattering the entire journey, high-pitched and completely incomprehensible to the other occupants of the Daimler. Every so often she would direct an especial leer in June's direction, wagging her finger and winking exaggeratedly. 'I sheen you beshore shumwhere . . .'

'You've seen June on the television, many times, Cynthia, my dear,' the Director General had eventually explained, sighing heavily. That was after the eleventh time that she had said it. The memory of Cynthia, slipping down the staircase in her sequined gown, returned to June each time. What a lot had happened since then. She wondered if Blossom wasn't beginning to long for a brief respite from the life of the career-woman, whether she might have liked to stay on down here for a while as herself. They hadn't really talked about that. As for herself, she was quite content whichever way it went. She loved either life – knowing that each was at her disposal. Tonight, on the walls of the Art Gallery, hung three of her large seascapes. Blossom hadn't seen those yet, it was to be a surprise. Tonight, apart from being the Fancy Dress Ball, was the official opening of the Society's New Year Exhibition. June looked forward to Blossom's reaction. She only hoped that the Director General's Daimler would not arrive much later than Blossom and Randolph, otherwise the tricky situation might occur of someone congratulating Blossom on paintings that she had no idea existed!

In fact, since Randolph insisted on parking his car in the garage, knowing full well that he would be incapable of doing so later, June made her Tweedledum entrance before Blossom and Randy. They were stumbling from the garage along the dimly lit cobbled street. The Gallery was situated in the very oldest part of Puddlemouth, there being barely room for the Daimler to even pass along the alleyway at some points. In view of this the chauffeurs parked a short distance from the Gallery and everyone at the end of the evening (whenever that occurred) would walk that short step to be driven back. June, of course would remain in Puddlemouth.

It had been difficult persuading the Director General (on Blossom's behalf) that she would really rather not travel back to London tomorrow with him in the Daimler. She very much preferred going on the train, and in any case with Cynthia in the car as well . . . He had regretfully accepted her decision. The real reason was that little Zachary Ram was meeting Blossom's train. Both she and June had felt rather guilty over Zachary. Neither of them felt that he had got much of a look in over Christmas. Though June had one sweaty session in the privacy of her bedroom with him after lunch on boxing day. Afterwards she and Blossom had compared notes on the impressive length (and width) of his cock. Blossom conceding to her sister, since she was the one who had last seen it, that when extended the whole thing reached up past the navel. Blossom harboured doubts about this, whilst granting that it would be easy to gain that impression. After all, Zachary Ram was quite a little person and it could be argued that the distance up to his navel was less than a larger person's anyway. It was a pretty hefty weapon either way. Both girls agreed that it was a wonder its owner didn't walk with a stoop, with all that weight hanging down in his drawers.

'If someone thought of tying a broom-head to his handle, he could double-up on his job as a street-sweeper on his way to work –' June began saying against Blossom's guffaws.

'Yeah –' they continued together, spluttering exactly the same thing. 'Without even having to bend over – ha,ha,ha,!' Their gaiety was contagious.

By the time everyone had deposited their coats, and made small and quite unnecessary repairs to their make-up, it was almost twenty minutes to twelve. There would be a bar extension through to two o'clock in the morning, so there was no fear of not being able to get a drink. Even so, everyone wished to have a full glass in their hand by the time midnight was striking. 'Wozzont shat she pointa –' Cynthia kept saying, rather aggressively. 'Chew haff a lill chink for Snew Yere!'

No one could begin to guess what she had come as, but part of her fancy-dress consisted of her wearing a white bath-towel, wrapped around the bodice of her very expensive evening gown. That and an alarming amount of scarlet lipstick applied to the tip of her finely chiselled nose. June, feeling a pang of conscience, thought that someone ought to be doing something about Cynthia. She looked ridiculous, presenting herself thus – perhaps the lipstick on her nose had been intended for her mouth. 'You tell her,' June urged Blossom, whilst they were still in the cloakroom, 'and for Christ's sake take that towel off her as well. She wouldn't look too bad without those.'

But it was not to be. 'You have lipstick on your nose, I think, unless I am very much mistaken.' Blossom had ventured politely, attempting at the same time to loosen the towel.

Cynthia had spun round viciously, clutching the towel in talon-like claws. 'Shmine!' Then she had glared at Blossom through meanly narrowed eyes, thrusting her face forward like a ferocious rodent. 'I sheen you beshore shumwhere . . .'

The girls gave it up as a bad job.

'Come on Bloss – I've something to show you.' June led the way to the far end of the gallery where her three large seascapes occupied one of the most important walls of the exhibition. But others had already beaten her to it. Standing in an admiring group before the paintings were Randolph, Emily Shawl, Bodmin Basil, and, rubbing his hands together with great delight and appreciation – the Director General.

They all turned at the approach of the twins. Randolph had two full glasses in his hand, one for himself and one for Blossom.

The Director General had been similarly thoughtful. 'Your drink, my dear.' He had neglected to bring one along for his wife, secure in the knowledge that she would head straight for the bar. June stepped forward, smiling so warmly that his old heart somersaulted crazily against his ribs.

Randolph held a glass toward the twin standing behind. 'Blossom,' his eyes twinkled, 'a fabulous start for the New Year – you have just made your first professional sale!' And he lifted his own glass toward the nearest seascape. The Director General had purchased the painting for the foyer of Television Tower, it was exactly what was needed in that concrete monstrosity. They had been looking for just this sort of breath of the elements, this glorious burst of vitality for a long time . . . Bodmin Basil endorsed his opinion and not to be outdone he bought the second of the three paintings. He had the ideal space in his house, he knew the wall. Between the windows in the dining room, with the westerly view of the moors . . . Emily Shawl sidled up with her box of tiny red stars in her hand and, biding her time, waiting for the most suitable pause in the conversation, she announced that the Selection Committee of the Puddlemouth Society of Arts had chosen to purchase a Blossom Tree seascape as one of their annual acquisitions for their Permanent Collection of Members' Works . . .

With four minutes to go to the striking of midnight June Day had sold one thousand, five hundred pounds' worth of painting. A bewildered Blossom received all the congratulations.

Midnight chimed. Two telephone calls from London to Puddlemouth were being cancelled out, not only by each other, but by a third from Prague, and a fourth from the University of Oxford. All four calls had been firm arrangements made between June (or Blossom standing in for June) and Lord Valentine, Zachary Ram, the Czech director, and Professor

Hamilton Hamilton. It was to be a secret, but each of the callers intended to make a proposal of marriage. Although at least two of them (Zachary Ram and the Czech) despised betrothal between human beings as the height of bourgeois mentality. Nevertheless this would be the intention of all — if there had been an answer to their call.

The thing was that June (and of course Blossom) had clean forgotten any such arrangement. And had they remembered, there was nothing that they could have done about it now.

As the chimes died away, after everybody had kissed everybody that it was possible to kiss, including kissing them twice if they happened to be handy — and then again if something special had accidentally been ignited — June stole out of the door. So did the Director General.

Cynthia was sozzled. She knew she was because, swaying here at the bar, she had begun to see double. However much she screwed up her eyes, however desperately she tried to focus — by closing first her left eye and the the other — she still kept seeing two instead of one. She was really searching for her husband, but there were so many people. Crowds that shouted around her, singing and linking arms in a ridiculous fashion. She thought she had seen him just a second ago. A person in baggy check trousers and what looked like a schoolboy's blazer had been beside him. The person had very short yellow hair with a little peaked cap sitting at the back of the head. And (this was where it began to be worrying) this person had their arms around another person who seemed to be the same person . . . Cynthia shut her eyes, blinked, then looked again. She was seeing double. There was no doubt about it. The thing to do was to steady herself with another little drink. She chose to drink brandy, although she had started the evening rather demurely on Champagne. Proceeding cautiously to Martinis, from them through to Bloody Marys. Then riproaring straight on to neat Scotch. She could probably do with a spot of fresh air, this was the trouble. There were too many people shoving and pushing. They were behaving like animals, it was absolutely monstrous . . . heaving all around her . . . she had to get out. Outside to some fresh air and to some sanity. A small sob broke in her throat as she wavered unsteadily through the boisterous revellers. Where was her husband? She needed him desperately, she needed him . . .

144

And then she saw him.

He was way ahead of her, as far she could see – he was pushing his way through in the direction of the door. Now he had
reached it. It was open already, the person ahead of him had
opened it. That person was the one with the yellow hair and the
little peaked cap. But now there was only one of her. Thank
God she had stopped seeing double! And thank God – it looked
as if they were going home.

The Director General was panting. It was extremely difficult
to walk in this wind, even with their arms around each other he
and June were finding it hard to stand upright. They had
rounded the corner that led down to the beach – a romantic
desire had swept over him – this was where he wished to make
love to his love – on the beach and under the stars. But there
were no stars, and there was barely a moon. The vast stretch of
the sky was heavy with scudding clouds racing across the thin
lemon light leaking through a shrouded crescent. The moon.
These were heavy gale conditions, there would be no boats out
tonight. The noise of the breaking surf was tumultuous in
their ears. And the Director General found himself responding
with an answering passion in his soul. This was the life! He
lifted his face to the ferocious heavens, savouring the salt spray
on his lips. Not looking, he stumbled. June held him tight.

'Be careful!' She warned. 'Best to look where you're going
here – there's a drop down there straight into the sea. I'm
taking us to a sheltered place I know.'

He followed her advice, humbly, consumed by his love.

Behind them unsteadily Cynthia followed too, consumed by
her irritation. What a fucking long way to the shitty
Daimler . . .

CHAPTER SIX

'Guess what.'

'What?'

'Just guess.'

'What – guess anything?'

'Yes – anything. Go ahead and guess anything you like about me.'

'Ah – about you! That's a clue. About you. I guess –'

'Yes – go on, guessing.'

'I guess about you – I know it – I guess that you, June Day (though still posing in Puddlemouth as Blossom Tree), are –'

'Yes? What?'

'Are pregnant!'

'Oh Bloss –' June was disappointed, she had wanted to say it herself, not be told like this. 'How did you guess!?'

Blossom laughed into the telephone. 'Well, my darling, it was only a guess. But are you really? But that's wonderful, absolutely smashing! Christ, you must be thrilled! Have you told Randy yet? What does he say? When is it due? Ooh, I shall be able to be godmother!'

There was silence at the end of the line.

Blossom burbled on, heedlessly. 'Well, it is about time – let's face it. Every woman,' she assumed a purposely pompous voice, 'should experience the wonder of childbirth.' Eventually she realised that something was wrong and then she expressed her concern.

'I haven't told Randy yet because,' June responded slowly to Blossom's anxious promptings, 'because for one thing I wasn't certain till this morning. I got the results in the post from one of those Pregnancy Advisory addresses. I thought it wiser to do it that way than go to this new doctor down here.'

'Clever thinking,' Blossom spoke gently. She could tell that June was really upset. But why? With her sort of news she should be the happiest girl in the world.

'Yes. Although I sort of *knew* that I was pregnant – you do, don't you. Remember when you said you knew even before the poke was over that you had conceived Pip?'

'Yes, that's right, I did. Is that what happened with you? I mean can you actually trace it back to a particular screw?'

'Would that I could!' June wailed, raising her voice. 'You're not working it out are you . . .'

The facts of the matter were that ever since June had settled into the life-switch, really settled in, the idea of having a baby had appealed to her more and more. The set-up was so perfect, besides which she had waited long enough. It had never been her intention to travel through life childless, so why not start now? If she and Tiny had stayed together, a child had been one of the next items on the agenda. That had been the main regret when they had split up – that having a child would have to be postponed. If she didn't look out she would be leaving it too late.

But she hadn't told anybody that this was in her mind. Not even Blossom, particularly not Blossom. The reason being that she felt that it would be a form of blackmail, a way of preventing Blossom from returning to being herself (if she had wished to). June felt this very strongly. She didn't want it to look as though she was planning to stay for ever and ever. The whole thing needed to be open-ended at all times. It wasn't as if she had relinquished her career anyway, she still had it in mind to return to being the (now) very celebrated June Day. But it was just that of late she had been feeling exceptionally broody. She found herself unexpectedly peering into prams parked outside shops. For no reason at all she had purchased a tiny and exquisite Victorian christening robe – and had hidden it so that no one should see. It was ridiculous.

It was more than that, it was ridiculous and it was irresponsible. Two months running, in October *and* in December, she had inadvertently forgotten to take her Pill! This was something that she had never, ever done. Waiting for the first period to appear after the October carelessness had been a nail-biting time of wild delight and deep disappointment. She had been half a day late, by her hysterical calculations. And was already engrossing herself in the 'Naming the Baby' chapter of *The Guinness Book of Names*, secretly of course, when she had felt the all too familiar rush of moistness flooding into her knickers. At the sight of the scarlet stain she had collapsed on the lavatory seat and wept. She hadn't realised until that moment how much she had wanted a child.

Even so, in November, she had taken careful precautions. After all it wasn't up to her to decide, just like that, to become pregnant. Surely the father had some say in the matter. If she were anything of a woman she would discuss it all round. First talk to Blossom – it surprised her that her sister hadn't brought the subject up herself. They more often than not conducted their thoughts along the same lines. The fact that Blossom hadn't mentioned it inhibited June from doing so. She supposed she would come round to it all in good time.

But in December exactly the same thing had happened all over again! This time June accepted that what she was doing was not even sub-conscious any more. What was worse was that it was not only once, but *three times*, on three successive mornings that she didn't take the Pill. And she had played a childish game with herself, pretending to be confused. Pretending that she had taken it, yet at the same time not checking up, not going to look even at the clear evidence on the sheet of pills. It was as if she were a gambler trapped in her own obsession. She was risking it, only risking it. This was her reasoning. Anyhow, whoever heard of anybody becoming pregnant after missing one pill (OK, three pills)? Hadn't statistics proved that it was virtually a million to one chance of this happening? So if she did happen to turn out to be that one, rather than the million, then the whole thing must be in the hands of fate. She was *meant* to conceive. This baby had been preordained – if it became a reality under such circumstance.

This was the way that June looked at it.

But something else had motivated this reckless behaviour – the knowledge that the team of lovers would be down. Knowing that instead of one man making love to her (Randy), there would now be five more – surely one of the sexy buggers would score a bulls-eye!

But now she was in a state of confusion. She desperately needed Blossom to tell her what to think.

'Fucking arseholes!' Had been Blossom's first wise comment on fully realizing the implications. Her second reaction had been to laugh. And laugh. It had been minutes before she had been able to speak again. By which time June had begun to see the funny side too.

'Very few people would believe this, you know, kid –' Blossom chuckled happily. 'A choice of six as to who is the father. Well, my darling, it's up to you. Every single one of them has proposed already. So it can't be said to be a shotgun wedding can it, whoever you choose – rather neat that. I must say that you have timed it a treat. Well, which one do you think? I'm afraid I can't be of any help at all. I wouldn't be able to choose, I haven't any favourites between them, have you? I think they're all absolutely gorgeous. Of course,' her voice became thoughtful, 'there are other alternatives. You could stay with Randy, I mean the baby could be his. It's a one in six chance – very low odds for anyone with a betting streak . . .'

June interrupted and spoke in a rush. 'That's the thing – I couldn't do that. I couldn't stay and have the baby. He's made an appointment this week for a vasectomy. He told me last night. He said he'd been thinking about it for a long time and now he's made up his mind. He says that we've enough children, no responsible person should foist more than two on the world. And that since we've got one of each anyway – both of them little sods, he said, but I'm sure he was only joking, you know how he does go on about them – anyway what he finished by saying was that the very last thing he wanted around the house was another stinking bundle of swaddling clothes, forever shitting out of one end and squalling out of the other. I had no idea that he felt so vicious about small babies – he was really vituperative!'

Blossom gave a long drawn-out sigh. 'I must admit that I'd forgotten. Yes. I'm afraid it's all coming back. He did rather loathe Pip and Willow when they were babies. Lots of men do. And of course they did disturb the nights, he was positively childish about that. I didn't ever tell anyone but did you know that one morning he put Pip in the dustbin. After a really terrible night when the poor little thing was teething and we hadn't had more than an hour of sleep all night. But can you imagine a grown man doing that! And the child's father too! Honestly it nearly split the marriage in two, I can tell you. I very nearly left him over that. There I was running around like a thing demented when I found the pram empty outside the front door. I mean I only looked in the dustbin because I wasn't myself and anywhere seemed possible – I even looked down the lavatory. That would have been a better place, that's what I screamed at him afterwards. Then, I said, the brute could have flushed the little thing straight into the sewers, no evidence. As it was, I was only just in time with the dustbin. The refuse cart was almost with us. It was just there at the top of the road – can you imagine! And the bastard would have let me believe that the baby had been snatched by one of those baby-snatchers. There had been a lot about them in the news at the time, which is what had given him the idea. Of course, he was going through a bad time with his work around then. A small crying baby doesn't go with deep concentration, I must say.'

Both girls decided that staying on with Randolph would be a very bad idea. Hey-ho, time for another switch . . .

It was inconvenient that week. Momentous things were happening in June Day's career. She had been tipped as the likeliest successor to the nice and late lamented Nobs Plater. Yes – it was thought that the all-important position of prime newscaster for Universal Television should now be given to a woman. June Day was on a short list of seven. This week should be the decider. It was being put to the nation to choose their own newscaster. The situation was absolutely unprecedented.

A master-plan had been devised whereby all seven finalists should be given the Ten o'clock News to read. One a night. Thus providing viewers with the opportunity of seeing each of the candidates for the job in fair and unprejudiced conditions. A national poll would be conducted to discover the public's choice. The findings of which would be made known by the end of the day. It would be conducted exactly like a political event, just the same as the general election, with similar polling booths set up all over the country, hourly reports taking place on the television. Even at this point, before all the candidates had taken their turn, the betting shops were doing brisk business. June Day was already ahead of the rest – clear favourite with odds at two-to-one. Tomorrow, Wednesday night, would be her turn at ten o'clock. Although her detractors claimed that giving her a Wednesday night would be unfairly to her advantage since it was the one night that the masses watched the box – her supporters felt that she needed no such boost. Her popularity placed her automatically ahead.

She won.

CHAPTER SEVEN

Blossom Tree signed her name with a flourish at the bottom of her canvas, then she stood back to admire the painting. She had been worried that it wouldn't be dry in time for collection. Tomorrow all twenty of her works were being driven to The Sliced Eye Gallery in London. Her first one-woman exhibition would be opening on Monday. The whole family would be going up for the private view.

It was still difficult to regard herself as a professional (and financially successful) artist. June was the one who had started the ball rolling with her wonderful seascapes. Everything had taken off when the seascape bought by the Director General, had been so ceremoniously hung in the foyer of Television Tower. So many people had come to the party! Including – and this was what really had done it – the Art critic of *The News*. Zachary Ram had brought him along. Sweet thing. And the following Sunday the critic had made lengthy mention of the 'exuberant and absolutely splendid painting – the sea-spray flies from the canvas, of the Cornish artist, Ms Blossom Tree, wife of the famous philosopher Randolph Tree, and sister of television star Ms June Day'.

And then the London Galleries had descended.

It had been rather awkward really, all of them wanting to see her new sea-scapes. There weren't any new ones. Nor were there likely to be. Blossom was back, being Blossom, and try as she might she had been unable to find inspiration in the sea. Nudes were what she liked painting, nudes in the abstract with a touch of surrealism. The nearest that she could approach the sea in her work were her mermaids. She had plenty of those if anyone was interested.

The Sliced Eye Gallery in Soho was very interested indeed.

Blossom yawned. She was tired, it was almost ten o'clock. Good. June would be on in a minute.

151

It was lovely to be able to see June every day like this. To be able to watch her getting bigger every day. One more month, that was all till the baby's birth – the most publicised birth since Princess Anne had hers. And yet how the revelation of June Day's pregnancy had rent the nation in two only five months ago.

An unmarried mother reading the British news!

It had made headlines, and not just in this country. Many women everywhere sprang up in fierce defence of June Day. What courage, what honour, what pride and what bravery. June Day epitomised the position of her sex today. She was a champion. She was a cause. She was an example.

There was no way that she could have lost her job.

No one knew who the father was. In outrageous interviews of staggering candour June Day admitted as much. She had been, so she proudly announced, to bed with five (she and Blossom agreed to leave mention of a sixth out of this. Randolph was not too stupid to put two and two together) different men during the month that she had conceived. There was no way of knowing who the father might be. She had explained this to the gentlemen concerned. No she would prefer not to give their names, however if they themselves wished to reveal their identity then she had no objection. It was really up to them . . .

Her revelations, her flabbergasting revelations, made her the hottest property on television. The viewing ratings for the Ten o'clock News every night were the highest ever recorded for any single programme in the entire history of the medium. The rival station could do nothing, they were helpless. And the programmes either side of the news suffered too. The rivals made a colossal bid for her services. The figure mentioned was 'astronomical'. In panic her own employers made a similar offer simply to keep her with them. For the next six months at least June Day would be top news.

And when she had had the baby – well it wouldn't end there. She had already stated that not only did she have every intention of resuming work as soon as she was able. But that she looked forward to having a large and happy family. She might even get married one day to one of her five gentlemen – they all seemed perfectly content to wait. Her child would be regarded as belonging, one fifth, to each and every one of them. Not

every child was fortunate enough to be blessed with so many ac-
knowledged fathers . . .

CHAPTER EIGHT

Randolph Tree kissed his wife's nipples slowly and with great love. She had been away from him for a week collecting June's children for a visit and he had missed her very much. In that time he had practised the habits of a monk. By the time of her return he had been ready to explode. For the very first time in their married life they had beaten their own record. He was forty-five and he had just fucked his wife ten times within twenty-four hours.

'You are my life,' he whispered to her tenderly.

'And you are mine,' she whispered back.

This was true. He was her life. Well, he was really, as much as any man. So June thought. But then that was how it should be – she and Blossom sharing everything as they always had. And as they would continue to do.

The door of the bedroom swung open. Two small boys stood there, two absolutely identical children. June's twin sons. 'Blossom – your nephews.' Randolph smiled at the little bastards, knowing perfectly well that he was their father.